TWO
SUMMERS

Also by Glenn Patterson

FICTION
Burning Your Own
Fat Lad
Black Night at Big Thunder Mountain
The International
Number 5
That Which Was
The Third Party
The Mill for Grinding Old People Young
The Rest Just Follows
Gull
Where Are We Now?

NON-FICTION
Lapsed Protestant
Once Upon a Hill: Love in Troubled Times
Here's Me Here
Backstop Land
The Last Irish Question: Will Six into Twenty-six Ever Go?

TWO SUMMERS

Glenn Patterson

NEW ISLAND

TWO SUMMERS
First published in 2023 by
New Island Books
Glenshesk House
10 Richview Office Park
Clonskeagh
Dublin D14 V8C4
Republic of Ireland
www.newisland.ie

Print ISBN: 978-1-84840-898-2
eBook ISBN: 978-1-84840-899-9

Typeset by JVR Creative India
Cover design by Niall McCormack, hitone.ie
Printed by L&C, Poland, lcprinting.eu

New Island receives financial assistance from the Arts Council/an Chomhairle Ealaíon and the Arts Council of Northern Ireland.

New Island Books is a member of Publishing Ireland.
Set in Adobe Caslon Pro in 12 pt on 17 pt

10 9 8 7 6 5 4 3 2 1

For the sweepers and the singers

Contents

Summer on the Road

THAT WAS THE SUMMER Mark was sleeping on the sun lounger in the front room. Jilly had come home from Edinburgh the week after Easter with Danielle. Second time since the New Year.

'I'm not going back this time,' she said. She said that the last time too. Then she had stayed less than a week, most of it out in the hall on the phone, Danielle on the floor at her feet playing with whatever the telephone seat drawer yielded up by way of toys: neighbours' spare keys, Goodwill Offering envelopes for Sunday services long since passed, squirmy elastic bands that Jilly said were a choking hazard and shouldn't be there.

'They shouldn't be there?' her father said. '*They* shouldn't be there?'

He didn't finish. He rarely did.

Jilly went back to Edinburgh and three months later came home again. Ten weeks now and counting.

She had had the box room when they were growing up, being the eldest, being the girl. Her room had been off limits to Mark and Dennis, the only door in the house other than the bathroom door, facing it down the landing, that was ever shut.

Which only seemed to make her more paranoid.

'Which one of yous was in my room?' she would say at dinner.

'It wasn't me.' (Mark)

'It wasn't me.' (Dennis)

'It was me.' (Mother) 'I had to put away your ironing.'

'I could have put it away myself.'

'The last lot was still sitting on top of the chest of drawers.'

'I've been busy, in case you hadn't noticed.'

Mark didn't know about Dennis, but he did go in there sometimes, those very rare occasions when there was nobody else in the house, on the lookout for magazines – between the mattress and the bed base, the more grown-up ones were – hands sweating as he searched them for the problem pages.

My boyfriend says if I loved him I'd go all the way.

I am embarrassed by my hair you know where.

I am seventeen and still haven't had my first period.

Are you really supposed to *blow*?

Jilly clearly couldn't go back into the box room, not with Danielle, and the travel cot (it weighed a ton when he carried it up the stairs for her) and all the other bits and pieces it took to keep a baby of fourteen months going from one day to the next.

The original plan was Mark and Dennis would alternate on the sun lounger, till Dennis said, 'Well wait a minute: I've my O levels coming up. Nobody made Mark sleep on a sun lounger last year.'

'Sure, why would they have? Jilly wasn't here last year.'

'It doesn't matter: nobody made you.'

'He has a point,' their father said and nodded.

'Oh, listen, if I'm making everybody's life difficult,' Jilly said.

'You're not,' said their mother. 'Mark can sleep on the lounger on school nights and Dennis can sleep on it at the weekends. There.'

'I have to revise at the weekends too you know,' Dennis said. He had his head down, but Mark knew he was smiling: he had hardly had a book in his hand all year.

'You can swap as soon as the exams finish,' said King Solomon, in their father's voice but then midway through June a friend of his whose wife worked in the City Hall told him of openings in the Council's cleansing department – holiday cover for roadsweepers and binmen – and without even talking to Mark about it he said sure, why not, put his name down.

'I thought it'd be money towards when he goes to university,' he told Mark's mother, the day the letter dropped on the mat with word – the first anyone else in the family had heard about it – that Mark had been offered the job, starting first Monday of July. 'And he'll get a donkey jacket out of it.' Which, since it sounded as though he wasn't going to get to hold on to much of the money, was actually the one detail of the deal Mark could see in his favour.

'Now, the only thing is, the depot they have assigned you is over the far side of the Shankill Road.'

'The Shankill! What time does he have to start?'

'Half seven.'

'He'll have to be leaving here about quarter past six if he's to be there on time. It's two buses.'

'Does that mean I'm going to be woken up every morning with him clomping through the living room?' Dennis said. 'Some rest that's going to be for me!'

'He has a point,' said their father.

So Mark was sleeping in a sleeping bag on the sun lounger. Or not sleeping a whole lot. There were the springs for one thing. Twelve of them in all. Thick and hard and, after even a minute or two away from direct sunlight, cold. They really only left you a strip up the middle about two feet wide to lie on.

And then there was Danielle.

Some babies woke smiling no matter what hour of the day or night, his mother said, and some babies never woke but they howled. 'I had two smiley babies and one howler – you – in between, which just goes to show you.'

Don't be too hard on the wee thing, in other words, even if she's doing her howling right above your head at five o'clock when you have to be up in an hour for your first day at work.

He was up and dressed, in the end, twenty minutes before his alarm was due to go off. He had washed the night before so that he wouldn't have to go up the stairs, though how any of the rest of them slept through Danielle's waking and being changed and put back down again for another hour or two – 'please, for Mummy' – was beyond him.

His mother had left him out two pieces of bread buttered side up on a sheet of tinfoil and a bowl beside them with sliced tomato in it. Next to the bowl she had left a piece of paper with the address of his Great-Aunt Irene ('round corner from old place', she had added in brackets), though as his father had already said she was on the other side of the Shankill entirely, and it wasn't as if Mark was going to have time in his day to just dander across there and say hello.

He made up the sandwich and put it in the pocket of his bomber jacket and let himself out by the back door.

He passed a wee lad out on his bike delivering the early morning papers, but apart from him, and the far-off whine of the milk float, stopping and starting, stopping and starting, no one appeared to be out and about. Not even the fellas who boasted about sitting out all night to guard the Eleventh Night bonfire, on the waste ground at the entrance to the estate.

The estate was on a Blue Bus route, which meant it was technically outside the city limits. The first bus didn't leave until seven o'clock. The stop for the Red Bus – the City Bus – was another fifteen minutes' walk through the estate next to his. Half a dozen people were waiting, all in their own wee worlds, though they turned as one when he joined them on the footpath, almost as though he had gatecrashed a party. The bus, coming from a third estate, was a single-decker, a quarter full, mostly down at the back in the smoking seats. Mark stood near the front in the space for baby buggies, hanging on to the strap and watching the suburbs gather themselves into the city proper. Still the only shops open were newsagents and petrol stations, but at every stop more people got on, so that by the time the bus pulled up at the side of the City Hall, Mark was pressed right up against the window.

He had to pass inside the security gates on to Donegall Place to catch his second bus. It was nearly always civilian searchers these days, with just a couple of soldiers standing behind chatting to each other. A couple of Rag Days back, four men in fancy dress had stepped out from the students throwing flour at passers-by and shot a soldier and a woman searcher at the gate near the cathedral.

Mark saw himself in the angled mirror above the way out raise his arms while a searcher waved a wand vaguely about his legs and up his back. A second guy patted him down. Came back to his jacket pocket for a second pat. (His *bomber* jacket, for fuck sake.) A squeeze.

'What's that in there?' he asked.

'My lunch,' Mark said and went to take it out, but the guy shook his head: on you go.

Two Rag Days ago: aeons.

A church bell (where was it?) was chiming for seven o'clock as the second bus – another single-decker – pulled in. Again Mark stayed near the front, further forward in fact and not for the view this time. He was less certain of his fellow passengers, where they were coming from and where they were getting off. The route passed through Carlisle Circus – Shankill on the left side, New Lodge on the right: Protestant, Catholic, you might as well say – and then up the Crumlin Road, between the courthouse and the jail, as far as Agnes Street on the Shankill side, which was where Mark had been told he should get off. After that he didn't know: Oldpark, maybe, or Ardoyne, both places he had grown up understanding he ought to avoid.

Of course nobody said a word of any sort to him.

As he was standing waiting to cross the road though, a wee girl sitting on the back seat next to her mother gave him the fingers up the side of her nose.

Then the bus pulled away and he was looking up the long street of three-storey houses that led to the Council depot.

He zipped up his bomber jacket and jogged across.

First thing he noticed when he reached the end of the terrace were the bullet holes in the pillars supporting the corrugated iron gates. You could nearly have drawn a straight line joining the holes on the left and the holes on the right. He remembered as a kid making a machine gun out of fists held one in front of the other, sweeping them from side to side: *dow-dow-dow-dow-da-dow-dow-dow-da*.

'M60.' A fella in Council overalls was coming up behind him. Must have seen Mark looking. (He hadn't actually made those fists, had he?) What little hair the fellow had was golden in the early morning. A barley field after harvest. 'Year before last. Provos took over a house just across the peace line there.'

The 'peace line there' consisted of more corrugated iron with, on this side of it, hymns to the UVF and *FUCK THE IRA*.

'Bastards.' Another, ganglier skinhead fell in beside. 'You one of the summer boys?' he asked Mark. 'What school are you at?'

'Methody.'

'Hear that, Tony? Fucking Methody.' He brushed the tip of his nose a couple of times with his index finger: *snooty, snooty.* 'Did you need an atlas to get here? A chauffeur?' He spat through his teeth. 'Fruit.'

'I have an aunt lives down the road,' Mark said. Great-aunt sounded too remote. Like other side of the Shankill entirely.

'Oh, yeah? What's her name?'

'Irene. Irene Bell.'

'Never heard of her. You heard of her, Tony?'

Tony shrugged. 'I know a whole load of Bells.'

The other skinhead cackled. 'Load of balls, you mean.' And he arched his back in anticipation of a toe up the arse that was never in the end aimed.

The depot – the yard – was about the size of the main quad at school, only instead of the assembly hall there was a garage for the bin lorries, instead of the sixth-form centre there was an open-fronted shed with street-sweeping carts in various shapes and sizes. The office was on the left, about where the staffroom would be.

'You'll need to see the foreman,' Tony told Mark.

'Samson!' The other skinhead rubbed his hands together. 'He'll put some manners on you, the same boy.'

'Fuck sake, Alec, leave the wee lad alone,' said Tony and the two of them went into the building by another door.

The corridor Mark found himself in smelled of bleach. More than bleach. It smelled of the place where all the other bleach in the world was made.

Two other boys were sitting at the end of it, three orange seats apart. Mark recognised the one farthest from him from the year above him at school. Funny name. Casper? One of the dope-smokers anyway. Early 70s throwbacks who had set their stoned faces against all recent musical trends. The world began and ended for them with Genesis. And lo it came to Trespass that with a Trick of the Tail the Lamb did on Broadway Lie Down. His features were squeezed into a three-inch strand of face between the tides of his centre-parted hair, which needed constant tugging and flicking to keep it from encroaching further. He tilted his chin a fraction in recognition.

'Is this where the foreman is?' Mark asked as he sat in the seat midway between him and the other boy.

'Supposed to be,' said Casper.

The other boy consulted his watch, black eyebrows knitting. 'It's only twenty-eight minutes past.' His voice hadn't so much broken as plummeted to the bottom of the well. He had the look of a rugby player – not schools rugby, one of those scrappers you saw on *Grandstand* on Saturday afternoons. Widnes v Warrington from Naughton Park. 'They told us half past.'

Two minutes later ('to the second' the big lad said out the corner of his mouth and from the very, very depths), the door opened and a man came in. He was not much over five foot tall, a stone at best for every foot, bald but for a couple of tufts above his ears. They appeared to have been dyed plum, the tufts on the left a shade lighter than the tufts on the right. He couldn't have been anyone but Samson.

'Grammar school boys are yous?' he asked. 'You know yous are taking men's jobs?' Mark, Casper and the big lad looked at one another. Holiday cover, that's what it had been described to them as. 'So who pulled the strings for you?'

The big lad put up his hand. 'I've been doing this the last two summers,' he said.

'Oh, aye, and where were you before?'

'Clara Street and Park Road.'

The foreman humphed, 'Nowhere you had to do any real work then.'

'When do we get our boots?' Casper asked. They all looked down at the sand-coloured desert boots sticking out from the ends of his cord flares.

'You want boots?' the foreman took a step towards him so that they were nearly eye (standing) to (seated) eye. 'You'll get them when you've been here six weeks. Same goes for your donkey jacket and overalls. There were men walking out of here at the end of their first day all kitted out and then never coming back again. This yard must have dressed half the bucking Shankill. You'll see them yet – picked the letters off the back of jackets, of course, but I've got eyes, I see the outline: *BCC*. You know what that's for?'

Mark assumed he didn't intend the obvious answer.

'Before Charlie boy here Cottoned on.'

'BCBHCO,' Casper said under his breath.

Samson though had turned his attention to the big lad. He looked him up and down. Fruit of the Loom T-shirt, Wrangler jacket folded across his lap. 'Two summers you did? Where's all your gear, then?'

'I grew out of it,' he said, and the muscles under his T-shirt flexed.

'I might have bucking known.' Samson shook his head. He went into his office and came out with three pairs of gloves, gauntlets more like, deep cuffs and some sort of padding or reinforcement at the fingertips and knuckles. 'That's all yous are getting for now, and look after them. Any lost gloves you pay for yourselves. Understood?' They all three nodded. 'Come on, well, if you're coming.'

He brought them through to the room where the rest of the men were gathered. About twenty in all, late teens through to mid-sixties. Tony had taken out the *Sun* and folded it open at the sports pages. His skinhead friend – Alec – was trying to sneak a look at Page Three.

'Who's it the day? The Lovely Linda? Wee Dee?'

'How would I know?'

'Don't pretend that's not why you get it.'

'Right!' Samson shouted and jerked a thumb over his shoulder. 'These are your new playmates. Give them whatever help they need.'

'Us help them?' a man with no front teeth said. 'I thought they were supposed to be helping us.'

'I'm sorry to disappoint yous,' said Samson. 'Take it up with your MP, why don't you.'

Mark was put on a squad with Alec, who rolled his eyes and sighed, and an older man who got Benny after your man out of *Crossroads* because of his woolly hat. They crossed the yard with the other squads and stopped in the shed before a cart with worn wooden handles and a shovel lying lengthways between two metal brackets on the near side. A pair of brushes balanced on the top. The heads were a good eighteen inches wide. The bristles looked battle-hardened. Alec and Benny grabbed a brush each and walked off with them over their shoulders. Halfway to the gates Alec looked back to where Mark was still standing beside the cart.

'What do you want, an invitation? Come on to fuck!'

Mark took a hold of the handles and raised the cart's rear end off the ground – too high. The thing tipped forward on its two front wheels then, when he tried to get it back under control, veered off to the left and into another cart sending its brushes and shovel clattering to the floor.

Samson was showing the big lad – whose name it had now been decided *was* Big Lad – how the larger electric carts worked, pulling down on the lever sticking out from the front to start the motor. He turned to Mark. 'If you're not up to this, you know, I can walk out on to the road there and get someone who is, quick as that. There's hunderds would be glad of the chance.' He was practically levitating. '*Hunderds!*'

Over by the gates Alec and Benny were doubled up laughing.

Mark picked up the fallen tools, steadied the cart and pushed it across the yard and out the gates. The road down to the Crumlin Road – enough of a stretch when he had to walk it from the bus stop half an hour before – seemed twice as long. Alec and Benny had already crossed on to the Shankill side by the time he got to the end of it. Only for Benny's hat he wasn't sure he would have picked them up, turning into a street on the left.

They dropped their brush heads to the road, Alec on one side, Benny on the other, and set about the bits and pieces of rubbish along the gutters, stopping every ten or twelve feet when they had made a pile, a little swivel of the brush to neaten it up.

Mark set the cart down, unhitched the shovel and pushed it under the first pile without being bid. The dirt, the rubbish, went everywhere.

He stared in disbelief.

'Man, dear. You're meant to come at it from the side,' Benny said. 'Shovel in against the kerb.'

Mark was chasing after a Quencher wrapper he'd sent flying with his first attempt, trying to trap it with his foot.

'Never mind that,' said Alec. 'We'll get it tomorrow.'

Even coming at the piles from the side like Benny said, Mark lost about half of every shovelful between kerb and cart. Another street opened up on the right. Alec and Benny turned into it. Mark eventually followed behind. The piles were already waiting, but of Alec and Benny there was no sign. He started shovelling, all the time wondering where they had got to. Just short of the next junction he heard a whistle. Sounded like it came from the entry running at right angles to the street he had been working on. He looked in. No Alec or Benny. Then another whistle. A few yards in another entry opened, completely obscured from the street. He pushed the cart ahead of him round the corner.

Alec and Benny were standing leaning against the wall. They threw their brushes across the top of the cart as soon as Mark set it down then walked back down the alley, hands in their pockets.

'What are we doing now?' Mark called after them.

'Tea break,' Alec said. 'See you back here at eleven.' It was barely quarter past eight. He stopped at the corner. 'And for fuck sake make sure you keep out of sight.'

For two and three-quarter hours?

It crossed his mind to go and see his Great-Aunt Irene, but he had only the vaguest idea of where he was and next to no idea how to get from there to her street. While keeping out of sight. The only thing he could think to do in the end was to sit down against the wall next to the cart. At least the ground was dry. Warm too, surprisingly. He had been on the go from well before six. He was going to be on the go before six every weekday morning from now until he went back to school in September.

Six-a-fucking clock. *Six*-a-fucking *clock*.

Next thing he knew someone was kicking his foot. He leapt. Alec. He and Benny had their brushes over their shoulders. 'What do you think this is, fucking Butlin's?'

They headed back out on to the street they had already swept and turned off into the street cutting across it. The same kitchen houses, one window downstairs, two windows up, front doors opening directly on to the footpath. The same red tiled steps. They did that one and maybe five others, Alec and Benny brushing, Mark – with more success every street they went down – shovelling, before Benny and Alec threw their brushes across the top of the cart again.

'That's lunch,' Alec said.

'Do you want me to put the cart in one of the entries?'

'Why would you do that? Take it back to the yard. See you at half one on the dot.'

It must have taken him twenty minutes getting back. With all his struggles, it hadn't seemed at the time as though there was much going into the cart, but now – the weight of it – it was harder than ever to keep it balanced. As he passed between the broken line of bullet holes his arms felt as though they were being dragged right out of their sockets. The yard was deserted. Except for Samson.

'Empty your cart!' he yelled from the office doorway the second it came to rest. Mark walked around it with the shovel, wondering how the hell he was going to manage this. You'd have to stand on the bloody thing to get the right sort of leverage.

It didn't help that he had Samson watching him the whole time. Ah, fuck it. He had the shovel raised, the top of the handle a good foot and a half above his head when

Samson came walking across the yard and with his little finger lifted a tiny hook at the front of the cart. A door swung open.

'You tip the bucking stuff out,' he said and walked away.

So that's what Mark bucking did and only then did he reach into the pocket of his bomber jacket for his tomato sandwich … What was his mother thinking? What was he thinking? Tomato sandwich! Even before he unpeeled the tinfoil he could tell it was squashed. (The press of people on the bus into town. The double pat of the civilian searcher. All that raising and lowering of the cart.) A soggy red wedge.

He ate the drier, thicker end where he stood in the shed and threw the remainder in with the other rubbish. He only just had time for a slash before he had to pick up the cart and hightail it back to the Shankill. Alec and Benny sauntered round the corner a minute or two after he arrived. Stopped in their tracks.

'Where are the fucking brushes?' Alec said.

He had forgotten to put them back on the cart.

'We can't fucking work without brushes. Come on ahead, Benny.' And round the corner they went again.

The afternoon passed as the morning had. Nothing he did was right, or, if it was right, done on time. At one point he thought about just chucking down the shovel and walking away. Maybe all those men Samson gave out about who never came back after the first day weren't just motivated by the donkey jacket and boots. But where else was he going to get in now that the summer was started? And though university was still more a notion – a hazy one at that – than a definite plan, his father was right, he was going to need money whatever he did once school was ended, and he couldn't look to his parents for it.

He kept shovelling.

Big Lad was at the yard when he and Alec and Benny got back for knocking off, a couple of minutes before half past three. He had grown a beard since the morning, full and black. 'They sometimes make me go and shave at lunchtime in school,' he said. 'Apparently it unnerves the teachers.'

Casper arrived at that moment.

Alec pointed. 'Look at fucking Brainiac.'

His desert boots were lilac. He had picked up a discarded tin of emulsion paint only to find it wasn't as empty as it looked and had had a hole punched in the bottom.

'There's wee lads would put a hole in the bottom of a tin just for the laugh of it,' one of the other men said as they tipped out carts and returned them to the shed. 'You need to pick up the like of that with the handle of the brush.'

'And see plastic bags?' Alec added with relish. 'Shovel every time, or *phlttpp*' – he flicked out his fingers towards Casper's face – 'shite all over you.'

'They'd do that too all right for a laugh,' the other man said.

Mark caught the bus into town with Casper. (Trail of dimpled lilac prints all down the long road to the bus stop, all up the central aisle of the bus.) Not a word out of him until they were coming up to the security gates at the end of Royal Avenue.

'I hate those cunts,' he said then.

'They're just taking the piss out of us a bit,' Mark said.

A civilian searcher stepped on to the bus. Gave it the usual cursory once-over before staring at the footprints. The driver jerked a thumb over his shoulder. The searcher tilted her head until she picked out Casper's boots. She was laughing as she got off and the driver revved the engine again.

Casper shook his head. 'I do. I fucking hate them.'

'Well? How'd you get on?' His mother, across the table from him, addressed the question to Danielle sitting in her highchair at the far end.

Dinner times now revolved almost entirely around what Danielle would and would not eat. People made Os of their mouths (Mark felt himself do it, try as he might not to) as food was offered to her on the end of a fork, then closed them grimly as she palmed the fork away, scattering the cargo of Smash or sossies or Alphabetti Spaghetti.

'It was all right,' Mark said.

His mother opened her mouth. Closed it. Not this time.

'Where's your donkey jacket?' Dennis asked.

'You don't get them right away.'

'What, so it's like a promotion?'

'It's summer,' his father told Danielle, who had put her head down on top of her arms folded on the highchair's table. *No want!* 'Donkey jackets are more for the bad weather.'

Mark didn't bother to contradict him.

'So what did you get?' Dennis asked.

'Ten quid more in my pocket than you did sitting here at home.' He was rounding up.

'Is that what you're going to be getting, seriously? Fifty quid a week?'

Close enough. 'More if there's overtime.'

Dennis whistled. 'For pushing a brush around? Fair play.'

When he stripped off later in the bathroom his feet and ankles were black. His arms too, as far as his elbows. He pushed the rubber shower attachment on to the taps and stood in the bath hosing himself down, as he did most nights (he was too tired to do the other thing he did a lot of those nights). He didn't know how to explain it even to himself, but he felt as though he was not entirely the same person who had stood here last night.

Danielle went off at 5.35 am. He tried for a few minutes to get back to sleep, but it was no good. Besides, he had a plan. He ignored the slices of buttered bread and the banana his mother had left out for him and boiled an egg. Didn't matter what you did to a boiled egg, it would still be edible.

He ran it under the cold water tap till his fingers were numb, but even then – even with two sheets of kitchen paper around it – it was hot when he put it in his pocket. As he went to unlock the back door, he had another thought. He tiptoed up the stairs (snuffles only now from behind Jilly's door) and into the box room. Dennis sat bolt upright. Dennis aged six. Alfalfa hair. Blinking. (Seriously, how did he sleep through Danielle?) 'What's the matter?' he said or something halfway there.

'Nothing. Book.' Mark knew where the pile was, to the left of the doorframe, without having to switch on the light. He knocked the top book off by accident but grabbed hold of the one under that and curled it so it fitted into his other jacket pocket. Well, if he was going to be sitting around in an entry again for half the morning.

The silent partygoers turned again as one as he walked up to the bus stop, and as one looked away, half a heartbeat sooner than they did yesterday. Oh, you again. More room on the bus than yesterday too, he thought, from the vantage point of the same place he had stood then, even as they got closer to the centre of town: no one within a foot of him the entire journey.

Only as he was waiting to let other passengers off did he think about the egg. Fuck, they wouldn't have thought … He turned his head to the side and sniffed. Nah, they couldn't have. He sniffed again as he stood in the queue at the security gates. Watched the face of the searcher with the wand. (Not even a pat down today.) Then, as soon as he was out the other side, chucked the egg and its kitchen-roll wrapping away. Better safe than sorry.

He'd find a bakery and buy a sausage roll.

He had just crossed over the Crumlin Road from the bus stop when he saw Big Lad getting out the passenger door of a silver Audi up ahead, a hundred or so yards still from the Council yard.

Mark whistled. Big Lad spun round. Held up his hand. You could hardly have called it a wave. 'My dad works over this side of town,' he said when Mark caught up. (His dad was turning the car about double-quick time, reaching over to make sure the passenger door button was down.) 'It's on his way.'

They dandered along a while in silence.

'Actually, it's not really that close,' Big Lad said, 'but you know: dads.'

'Yeah,' said Mark. 'I know.'

Alec and some other fellas were playing pitch-and-toss up against the wall of the shed. Ten pees by the looks of it.

Alec was crouched, coin poised, when he saw them. 'Fancy your chances, lads?' he called.

'What do you think?' Mark said. 'For the sake of a couple of bob.'

Big Lad watched Alec's coin land. It was practically upright. 'Couple of bob? He'll skin us in seconds.'

Samson, though, came out of the office at that moment. 'You!' Mark? 'Yes, you; you're on the electric one the day. Big Lad, you take the handcart he had yesterday.'

Alec turned from the wall where he had been collecting his winnings. 'So, what, you make a mess of things you get a cushier shift?' It was the first time Mark had heard it stated that he had in fact made a mess. He blushed. 'How's that fucking fair?'

'What difference does it make to you?' said Samson. 'You still shove the brush the same way, don't you?"

'Shove it up your hole,' Alec said under his breath, 'bristles first.'

'I don't need to hear you to know what you're saying,' Samson shouted. Then to the yard in general, 'Like bucking Action Man, only has five sentences.'

'I'll tell what I have that Action Man doesn't have.' Alec grabbed a hold of himself by the balls, gave them a good shake. 'And you can ask your oul' woman that.'

'See?' said Samson. 'There's another of them!'

And he and Alec turned their backs on each other, both looking as though they thought they had come out on top.

Mark was sent out that morning with Tony and a fella by the name of Paul who looked to be the age Mark's granddad was when he died, only not in such good health. The electric cart was a doddle to operate all right, but it was big, heavy and, even flat out, slow. Mark imagined as he pulled down the handle to its 45-degree angle that he was taking a particularly docile rhino for a walk. Tony and Paul kept having to stop to let him catch up. They took the same route as Alec and Benny had yesterday only this time when they crossed over the Crumlin Road on to the Shankill side they took a right.

As had happened yesterday too they only did a couple of streets before turning into an entry and parking up the cart.

'See yous at eleven,' Paul said, a wave over his head as he carried on – coughing – down a connecting entry.

'What are you going to do?' Tony asked when he had gone.

Mark shrugged. 'Sit here probably.'

'Is that what you did yesterday?'

'I was dog tired. I have to be out of the house just after six to get my bus.'

Tony strained spit between his upper and lower teeth. 'You can come back to mine if you want, get some breakfast.'

Mark was about to say no, it was OK, it was a decent enough day and besides he had brought a book, but he had a whole summer ahead of him, rainy days as well as fine, and, like, the fella was standing there right in front of him, so, aye, all right, he said, if you're sure it's no bother.

'None at all.'

They mostly stuck to entries. It was hard for Mark to get his bearings. He glimpsed the odd street sign – Ambleside, did that say? – a church spire, a tall chimney starting to fall in on itself. Nothing he recognised.

Tony talked as they walked. There were always a couple of inspectors out, he said, but they had to cover all of north and west Belfast. Most of the time they didn't even bother getting out of their cars, so as long as you kept your cart well hidden you were fine.

They broke cover finally on a street with a shop on the corner. Tony went in and asked for a packet of bacon. The woman serving wrote it down in a pad hanging on a cord from a nail in the wall. Neither she nor Tony thought it worthy of comment.

Tony's house was round the next corner, in a row that had half a dozen bricked-up fronts. Blank dominoes among the spots. Mark had seen quite a few of them yesterday too: one entire street they passed down was deserted. The only sign that anyone had lived there the names and hearts written on the lamp posts and the bit of rope hanging off one that some kids had used for a swing.

Tony's door was open on to a porch about two feet deep. He pressed down on the handle of the frosted glass door at the end of it and at once – *Daddy! Daddy! Daddy!* – a couple of kids shot out and grabbed him by the legs.

Just seeing them with him put a few years on Tony in Mark's eyes.

'Easy on, easy on,' he was saying, 'say hello.'

The kids looked at Mark.

'What's your name?' the boy asked him.

'Mark. What's yours?'

'Fla-fla.'

'Don't you be cheeky,' Tony said. 'That' – a hand on the boy's head – 'is Frank, and this is his sister …'

'Fla-fla,' the girl said.

'Wow,' said Mark. 'Two Fla-flas in the one family, imagine.' And both children covered their mouths with their hands, laughing.

'Where's your mummy?' Tony asked.

A bigger child came halfway down the stairs. Eleven, twelve, knee socks, open-toed sandals. (Add another half a dozen years to Tony.)

'She's over in Auntie Sally's,' she said. 'These ones still weren't ready.'

'Are yous ready now?' Tony asked. The two Fla-flas showed him their shoes, all nicely buckled, their scrunch-eyed, scrubbed-clean faces. 'Well do you want to go on over too?'

Want to? They nearly knocked him and Mark down trying to get out the door. The older girl followed. 'Frank, Angela! Come here yous two and take my hand.'

'She's great with them,' Tony said. 'But boy, they have her tortured.'

He went ahead of Mark into the front room. 'Throw your jacket over the back of the chair there,' he said, although despite the age of the children he had just seen it didn't look to Mark like a room where anything had ever been thrown. Tony carried on through the curtain across the kitchen doorway and within minutes the smell of frying bacon and a little of the smoke from it drifted out.

'Put the telly on if you want,' he shouted above the sound of the kettle. 'See if there's anything on.'

It was too early in the morning for cricket and the English schools weren't off until the end of the month so there weren't even any kids' summer programmes on yet.

'Not a thing,' Mark called back.

'Stick the radio on then.' A transistor was propped up on the mantelpiece next to a brass carriage clock. Mark found the on–off dial. Tony came back through the curtain with a plate of bacon and another of pan bread already buttered. 'Make sure it's Radio 1. She has it tuned to that Downtown half the time. Who wants to hear people talking like us, right?'

He pulled out a little table with his foot from beside the settee while Mark hunted along the Medium Wave line for 247. 'Help yourself, I'll get the tea.'

The pot, like the cups and saucers and even the milk jug, was Pyrex, that colour that always made Mark think of egg whites just beginning to solidify in the pan.

They sat with plates on their laps, Tony in the armchair in front of the window, Mark in the one squeezed between fireplace and sofa. The breakfast show ended while they were still eating. Simon Bates came on.

'He's a smooth fucker, isn't he?' Tony said and did his voice. 'I promise you, this morning's Our Tune will really make you stop and think.'

They listened for a while trying to guess the year of the Golden Hour then Tony set down his cup and saucer on top of his plate. 'Think I'll have a bit of a kip here.'

Mark went to get up.

'Sit where you are, you're not bothering me.' Tony folded his arms and stretched his legs out in front of him, crossed at the ankles, so that the soles of his shoes were only inches from Mark's. A couple of minutes later he was snoring.

Mark must have waited another ten minutes before he dared move. He stepped over Tony's legs then bent to pick up the cups and plates and brought them through to the kitchen. The pan Tony had used was already washed and angled to drain on the rack. Nothing is left to sit, he thought. There was a practical side to all this tidiness. That was how space was made.

By putting away the washing-up liquid too, apparently.

He pulled back the curtain underneath the sink in search of it. Vim. Domestos. Pledge … No, it felt wrong to be poking around, even if he was trying to help. He let the curtain drop again and washed up using just hot water from a tank with a long slender tap mounted on the wall above the sink.

Tony had stopped snoring when he went back in, but if anything his sleep was deeper, chin tucked right into his chest, arms loose by his side. Mark tried closing his own eyes, but the way Tony's legs were sticking out he couldn't arrange himself comfortably enough in the armchair. After a couple more minutes turning this way and that he got up again and went looking for the toilet, though he knew there was only one place it could be.

He remembered, as he let himself out the back door, a summer when he was still in primary school, his father and his uncles making a roof out of Perspex sheets for his granny's yard, not so much bringing the toilet inside as bringing the inside out to meet her toilet. They had put a bath in too, or his Uncle Sid had, being the plumber in the family.

Not that it seemed to please Mark's granny. 'Nothing wrong with it the way it was,' she said. 'Yous're ashamed, that's what it is, afraid of your neighbours finding out that your mother still has to go outside – that *yous* used to go outside. Well, let me tell you …'

'You reared the four of us,' her sons said together.

'Well so I did,' his granny said, always said. 'And I'll tell you another thing, there weren't half as many colds and what have you when people were used with getting the air about them.'

'Freezing their you-know-whats off,' one of the uncles said and Mark's father nodded Mark's way as if he didn't know what your you-know-whats were or had never heard them called by their (im)proper names.

His granny would have held with Tony's yard all right: open to the elements, with a coal bunker against the wall closest to the back door (no coal or even coal dust this time of the year) and the toilet beyond. The toilet was as neat and tidy as the kitchen was and like the kitchen felt twice as big when you were standing within as seemed possible from without. The cistern was high up on the wall, a white china handle on the chain, and there was a framed sign over the toilet-roll holder on the left-hand wall. *If you sprinkle when you tinkle, please be sweet and wipe the seat.*

Mark flipped the seat up with the toe of his shoe but gave it a wipe anyway when he had lowered it again, in case any water had splashed up when he flushed.

He folded the square of toilet paper he had used very small. When he went to put it into the pedal bin, though, the bin was empty so he tucked it instead in the instep of his shoe. Simple.

As he closed the back door again behind him he noticed the key rack screwed on to the side of a cupboard. It had been carved out of a single piece of wood and varnished a deep mahogany. He tilted his head to make out the letters. *UVF LONG KESH.*

'Are you all right there?'

Mark started at the sound of Tony's voice from the front room.

'I just went to the toilet,' he said as he came back in.

Tony was sitting up straight now, a book open in his hand. 'This was sticking out of your coat pocket,' he said. 'I hope you don't mind.'

On the Road.

'Any good?'

Mark hadn't read enough yet to say for sure. It was meant to be good, he knew that. Jim Morrison had said so. Your man McCulloch from Echo & the Bunnymen said Jim Morrison was good. So …

'Absolute classic,' he told Tony.

He watched Tony's eyes run down a page, up, then down the page beside it. He flipped to the next pair. Ran his eyes down those and the pages after that. Whatever it was he was looking for (smut?) he didn't find it. He threw the book on top of Mark's jacket.

'Will we head on here then?'

He stepped out on to the street ahead of Mark. 'Pull the door behind you there, will you?'

Mark pulled the inside one, reached for the knocker of the outer door to close it too.

'Just leave that one. In case she doesn't have a key. It's all right, they're only round the corner.'

That afternoon Paul showed him how to take a brush for a walk, balancing the shaft on the middle finger joints of one open hand then twitching each finger in turn so that the brush head skipped along the footpath like one of those wee cocky terriers pulling on its lead.

'Here,' he said, 'give it a go.'

Mark did. Dropped the brush.

Paul wagged his head good-naturedly. 'It's harder than it looks.'

'Bishop.' It was a contraction they used at school for anything that came within half a mile of double entendre.

'Bishop?'

'You know, as the actress said to … Here, let me have another go.'

'Now you're getting it.'

Paul also explained that sweeping was not a push, but a pull. 'You push, all you're doing is spreading the dirt out. You want to bring it back towards you. See, like this.' It was, Mark recognised straight off, the same technique that Alec and Benny had used. 'I laugh my ballicks off when I see things on TV, *Play for Today* and all that, people sweeping out … it's an absolute joke. Whoever they have in to advise them obviously never lifted a brush in his life.'

'Wait, you think *Play for Today* has people in to advise them on sweeping?' Tony said.

'Why wouldn't they? They have people advising them on everything else.'

The hours flew in.

A couple of times as he worked Mark thought about the UVF key rack. It didn't have to be Tony's handiwork. Could have come from anywhere. A neighbour, a relative. There was that LP some Australian cousin bought when he was over visiting and left – by mistake? as a gift? he couldn't remember which – in Mark's mother and father's house. The No Surrender Band. Guns and accordions on the cover. (You'd be hard-pressed, listening to it, to say which were the most lethal.) It was still in the record cabinet, right at the back behind all the Mantovani and Bobby Crush and Dean Martin Live in Every Hole in the Wall on the American Continent that came with the record club they joined and then didn't know how to get out of.

Besides, he didn't suppose people who were actually in the UVF had things with UVF written on them or carved into them plastered all over their walls. Bit too much of a giveaway, say the police or the army ever came calling.

As they were crossing over the Crumlin Road at the end of the day they saw Alec, Benny and Big Lad (the bearded version) coming out of Agnes Street. Alec cupped his hands around his mouth. 'Here, Tony!' he yelled. 'You can keep that fucking student of yours – we'll take this one over him any day.'

'Don't mind that balloon,' Paul said, then nudged Mark. 'I don't like to tell you, but you have a bit of bog roll sticking out of your shoe.'

*

'That big bastard fired a used fanny pad at my head today,' Casper said, saving Mark the trouble of asking him how he'd got on with his crew.

There were bomb scares in town. Their bus was diverted round by the Albert Clock where it met the traffic from another alert on Oxford Street. The driver shouted down the bus that they might be as well getting out and walking.

Half the passengers instantly got up.

'What do you think?' Casper said.

River on one side, cordons on the other, the only way to walk would have been through the Markets, which on Mark's mental map of the city was tinted the same colour – green – as Oldpark and Ardoyne. (Or was it that he would show up Orange against it?)

'Let's just wait a minute and see.'

They waited, in the end, the best part of an hour, in the course of which the bus moved approximately twenty-five yards. At some point they heard the apologetic sound of a bomb-disposal charge going off. (Think of fireworks fizzing then failing to ignite.) An elderly man stood up and sang a song about Spanish eyes, until the younger woman with him managed to get him to sit down. 'I'm sorry,' she said, 'he's doting.'

There was another – louder – bang somewhere else in the city.

'That ought to do it,' the driver said and sure enough within ten minutes the roads were opening and the traffic was moving again at something registering in the miles per hour.

Mark wasn't home till nearly seven. Thirteen hours since he left the house. His mother met him at the back door.

'What kept you?'

'Bomb scares.'

'There was nothing on the news.'

'It's a nice day,' his father said. 'Somebody will have phoned in a warning just to get away from work early.'

'They shot themselves in the foot, if they did: the whole town was at a standstill.'

In other times and other places they might have been connoisseurs of tides, watchers of stars and clouds.

His mother wrapped a tea towel round her hand and opened the door of the grill compartment. She took out a dinner plate with another, smaller plate overturned on top. 'At least your dinner shouldn't be too dried out.'

She slipped a knife under the top plate, turned with it in her tea-towel hand to set it in the sink, turned back.

'What's the matter?' she said.

There was cabbage there and potatoes but all Mark could see was the bacon.

'Nothing,' he said. 'It all looks lovely.'

She and his father insisted on sitting with him, having a cup of tea, talking to him about his day: must have worked up a right appetite, all the same.

By the time he pushed back his plate he reckoned he was only one rasher off being declared officially hybrid.

When he went round to Tony's at tea break the next morning the kids were already gone. Probably all round at their Aunt Sally's, Tony said, before explaining that Aunt Sally wasn't really an aunt to anyone in the family – a cousin at several removes from his wife's father who had never married. She had something the matter with her thyroid and was more or less completely confined these days to her bed. Tony's wife, Brenda, was there as often as she was at her own house.

'Like, the woman has no one else belonging to her nearby,' Tony said, as though it stood to reason. 'And the kids love her. She's all these toys and things she's bought. The place is like a playground. Here she is, sure let them run about here all they like, it's not like I'm going to be using it much.'

He went into the kitchen and came back out with the Pyrex teapot and a plate of fruit soda toasted. They listened to the end of the breakfast show and the start of Simon Bates again.

Tony set his plate and cup down. Mark drew his legs back a few inches in anticipation of the pre-snooze stretch. Tony didn't move.

'Have you your book with you the day?' he said.

Mark did have, in the pocket where he had put it when they walked out the door together yesterday. He hadn't wanted to assume that Tony was going to invite him back to his a second time.

'Do you mind if I have a look at it again?'

He did the same thing Mark had seen him do the day before – running his eyes quickly down the pages, flicking over, running his eyes down the next two. He had done this half a dozen times before Mark realised he wasn't scanning on the hunt for smut or anything else – that was him actually reading.

He must have got through forty or fifty pages in fifteen minutes.

'I've seriously never seen anyone read that fast.'

Tony stopped and looked up. 'What? Oh, that.' He shrugged. 'I was like that at school. Our Karen's the same.' Karen? Sister? Or the girl on the stairs yesterday, perhaps? 'The teachers used to say to me, just you keep yourself amused there Bissett until the rest of these ones have caught up. Half the time I just went to sleep.' He grinned. 'I was always a quick sleeper too.'

He gave Mark his book back, but that was pretty much all he wanted to talk about the rest of the day, *On the Fucking Road*. 'I mean Dean, I can see what he sees in him all right, but like just to walk away and leave your kid – your baby – I think I'd have fucking lamped him. And that Terry one ...'

'Terry Dickson?' Paul said.

'A different Terry. You wouldn't know her.'

'Oh,' Paul raised his eyebrows. 'It's a her.'

'Seriously,' said Tony, 'what do you think's going on there?'

It had got way beyond the point where Mark could say he had never got further than the first few pages. Those questions he wasn't able to duck or deflect he tried to turn back. 'What do you think yourself?' Or, 'That's kind of what the book is doing, isn't it?'

Eventually he pulled the book out of his pocket again. 'Why don't you hang on to it?'

'Ah, no,' Tony said, 'that wouldn't be fair on you. Sure I can get it again tomorrow.'

A bit later he straightened up and clasped both hands on the brush handle. 'Oh, where is the girl I love?' he asked the street.

The street offered nothing in return.

Mark tried to read a bit on the bus, after he left Casper, to catch up, but only a couple of paragraphs in he felt his eyes start to go. He rubbed the corners. Concentrate. He wondered did he need to go back to the beginning. He folded the cover back on itself and the next thing he knew the bus was pulling up at the terminus two stops past his own. His cheek was stuck to the window. The book was on the floor, still open at the first page.

Thursday was payday. The men all came back to the yard at lunch and lined up at Samson's door to get their envelopes. He had none for Casper and Mark. (Big Lad, Mark only realised later, hadn't even bothered to join the queue.) 'It's your lying week,' Samson said in a voice like this is your left and this is your right. 'You've only done three and a bit days up to now.' He tapped a finger on one of the other pay packets. 'This isn't this week's pay, this is last week's. Yous'll get your this week's pay next and next week's pay the week after and the week after's the week after that. When you finish you'll get the pay for the week before the last one you worked.'

Casper cut across him. 'When do we get the pay for the last week then?'

'You get that at the same bucking time, of course.'

'Three and a bit days into that week.'

'That's right.'

'Which would be like paying us for this week this week.'

Samson sighed. 'No. This is your *lying week*.'

He looked like he was winding up to explaining it all over again.

'OK,' Mark said. 'Got it.'

Casper shifted his weight from one foot to the other. 'Could you maybe sub us a few quid?'

'Oh, wait.' Samson raised himself out of his seat, reaching for the wallet in his back pocket then sat again. 'No.'

'You didn't seriously think he was going to, did you?' Mark asked when they were out in the corridor.

'Thought it was worth a try. There's a guy waiting on eight quid from me. I told him I'd have it this weekend.'

'Could you explain to him that's for what you smoked this week so you'll pay him next week?'

Casper glanced at him past a waxing tide of hair.

'Come on,' said Mark. 'Eight quid dead? What else could it be for?' It was school quad mathematics: eight an eighth, sixteen a quarter, sixty-four an ounce.

Big Lad was standing with Tony in the lee of the shed when they went back out.

'Thanks for telling us,' Casper said.

'I thought you knew,' said Big Lad. 'I thought everybody knew.'

Mark looked about. The yard was practically empty. 'Where'd the rest of them go?'

'Pub probably,' Tony said.

'You not going?'

'Never had much of a taste for it.'

Mark had the taste all right, and the thirst: truly he could have murdered one or possibly several. What he didn't have – wouldn't have for another seven days – was the money.

'Oh, and I wouldn't be holding my breath waiting on them the rest of the afternoon,' said Tony.

It took Tony until Thursday of the next week – five and a half tea breaks – to finish *On the Road*. Mark had managed about a fifth of it in that time. If he was being honest, he didn't enjoy it all that much. If he was honest, he wasn't all that sold on Jim Morrison. As for your man McCulloch, he had only heard one Echo & the Bunnymen song. Rescue. It was all right.

He thought, as he ducked and deflected and turned back on themselves Tony's questions between the end of tea break and lunchtime, that he could have reached round the door of the box room in the dark that second morning and lifted any other book. What was the one that had fallen off the top of the pile? Spike Milligan maybe. *I rubbed my hands with glee. I always keep a tin of glee handy.*

'Have you listened to Duke Ellington?' Tony asked. 'I just always thought that was old people's music, but maybe it's not … And that book Sal's reading, what's it called?'

'Watch there till I shovel that.'

'Pr–, Pr– …'

The only thing that came into Mark's head was *Pride and Prejudice*. He very nearly, in his desperation, said it.

'Prowst, is that the way you say it? Proost?'

'That way.'

'What's that like?'

'It's like the longest book in the world.' Tony would probably have it finished in a fortnight. 'They say you should only read it in French.'

He knew, as he was saying it, that was low.

'That's me blown out then,' said Tony with a small shake of his head.

Mark was glad for more reasons than one that it was payday. Thirty-seven pounds sixty-three pence was all that his envelope contained: 'You're on the emergency code,' Samson told him. 'You can claim it back next April.' Even that couldn't put a dent in his good mood. Casper and Big Lad had already told them they were going to the bar with the rest of their squads as soon as they had collected their wages. He knew from last week that Tony wasn't much of a drinker. It wouldn't just be a pint he would be getting, it would be a respite. So up he went with Paul to meet the others in a place off Sidney Street West, leaving Tony standing in the yard.

The bar's only windows were high up on the front wall and covered with mesh. So much dirt had gathered in behind, it looked as though a bird might be nesting. The light from the open door barely reached the counter. In between that and the random flare of the fruit machine next to the toilets, the place was in shadow.

Mark heard, before he saw, that Casper and Big Lad were already in. Alec was winding the two of them up. 'Are you sure now yous know what to do with that? We call that a pint. Got that? A *pint*.'

He leaned forward out of the gloom suddenly, clocking Mark.

'Ah, fuck, here he is! Look, Larry, look, Curly, it's Moe!'

Benny shifted up a seat to let him sit next to his fellow Stooges while Paul went up to the bar. 'You're a student, for dear sake,' he said to Mark. 'Keep you your money in your pocket.'

That time of the day they had the place pretty much to themselves. An elderly man did come in at one stage and ordered a bottle of Guinness. He laid both hands flat on the counter between sips from the glass, staring dead ahead. When he was finished he took a hanky from his pocket and dabbed at something on the counter – a ring perhaps, where his glass had missed the beer mat – then wiped his mouth and left.

A short time later a young woman in navy stirrup trousers, bleached feathered hair, came in and bought a packet of cigarettes from the machine.

Alec called to her as she was leaving. 'Here, are you not speaking no more?' She sauntered over. His leg went out almost at a right angle, an invitation to sit on it, which she accepted, to his evident delight. He whispered something to her. She smiled. 'In your fucking dreams,' she said into his ear for all to hear and was up off his knee and away. He seemed as happy with that as with assent to whatever he had suggested.

Paul set a second pint in front of Mark. He didn't know where the third one came from, but he was halfway down it when a wee lad about ten stuck his head round the door and gave a long whistle. All around Mark men stood up and sank their pints.

'Inspector's car in the neighbourhood.'

'You know that by a whistle?'

'I know it by the wee lad doing the whistling.'

'But I thought as long as they didn't see our carts ...'

'Not on payday. They know where to look for us. Come on, drink up.'

'You've been drinking,' Jilly said when he landed in home. 'I can see it in your eyes.'

'I went for a pint.'

'At your age?'

'I'm coming eighteen.'

'Coming eighteen? You're barely turned seventeen.'

'That money is for your university,' his father said.

'It was one pint.'

'You're slurring.'

'I am not.' Actually he thought he might have been.

'She's only keeping you going.'

Jilly made a pinting motion with her right hand.

'I didn't even buy it,' he said.

His father asked him to sort out housekeeping with his mother.

'I thought it was for my university?'

'You can contribute something.'

'What are you looking at me for?' Jilly said.

'I wasn't,' said Mark.

'You were.'

'Oh, for fuck sake.' He slammed the living-room door on his way up to the bathroom.

'We'll have none of that sort of talk!' His father's voice carried through the plasterboard wall.

Dennis was standing on the landing when he came out of the bathroom. 'Lend us a tenner, would you?'

'A tenner? When are you going to pay me back?'

'I'll get money on my birthday.'

'*October?*'

'All right, before then.'

'What do you need it for anyway?'

'Going out.'

'Where to, the fucking Europa?'

Dennis shifted awkwardly. 'I'm seeing a girl.'

'You are?' It came out like a laugh.

'What's so funny?'

'It's not funny, it's just …' His wee brother was going out with somebody and he wasn't. 'Who is she?'

'You wouldn't know her.'

He was bluffing. 'Aye, dead on, you're seeing a girl.'

'All right, you call her Julie Warner. She's from Lisburn, Hillhall Road.'

'When were you ever in Lisburn?'

'I'm there every day while you're at work. While her ma and da are at work.'

Mark's stomach lurched. His wee brother wasn't

just going out with somebody, he was spending his days in bed with somebody. The most Mark had had was a couple of fumbles, back in fourth year. Tina Miskelly. She didn't even look at him now when she passed him in the corridor. 'I'm still able to get on the bus for a half most times,' Dennis said, 'but like five returns a week is rookying me. And then I've got to buy … Well, you know, we're there all day in the house on our own, so …'

Mark didn't want to hear any more. He pulled out the envelope from his back pocket.

'Here, here's five. Don't bother about paying me back.'

The only physical contact they had had with one another in the past ten years was brushing past on the stairs, the occasional shove in an argument, followed – very, very occasionally – by a grab for the head. 'Do you give in? Do you give in?'

Dennis looked at him as he might at a wardrobe he had to shift alone. Where to start? In the end he pulled the two ends of the fiver till it was taut.

'Cheers,' he said and went into the box room, shutting the door behind him. The wardrobe would keep for another day.

Mark looked into the envelope. Twenty pounds and some change. 'Fifty quid a week in your hand.' Yeah, right.

The next day was the Eleventh. The fellas guarding the bonfire at the entrance to the estate had got the hold of a brazier from somewhere. It smelled, as Mark passed it this last time, as though they had been trying to bake potatoes, and burnt them instead.

It had occurred to him a couple of times in the last ten days that there wasn't a big lot of bonfire building going on in the streets where he was working.

From the moment he crossed over the Crumlin Road that morning with Tony and Paul all he saw were kids dragging wood and other combustibles down to the street corners. Some of the piles were already over ten feet high.

'Where's it all come from?' Mark asked.

'They store it in the back yards, a lot of them, till the very last minute,' Tony said. 'Keep the other streets from burning theirs.'

'Aye, but these are only – what do you call it,' said Paul, 'you know – when people are learning to ski?'

'Nursery slopes?'

'Right. You want to see a fucking *Alp*, head on down to the bottom of the Road. That right, Tony?'

Tony shook his head. 'I don't know, I like the wee ones better. More the way I remember them when I was a kid.' He dropped the brush head to the ground. 'A hundred fucking years ago.'

It would be midnight before the bonfires were lit, but even at this early hour there was an air of carnival abroad. Every second door seemed to have music blaring out of it. There were Party tunes of course, the Sash, the Auld Orange Flute, but there was country and western too – or the Northern Ireland version of it – a bit of Quo, the *Grease* soundtrack, *oh yes indeeeed*.

People came out of their houses as they passed with their cart and handed them tips – coins for the most part though here and there a pound note too. 'Split that between yous.' A few handed them bottles of beer, clinked the bases with their own before toasting them. 'Good lads, good lads.'

Mark demonstrated taking the brush for a walk to a crowd of smallies who had been hanging around watching bigger kids finish putting up a bonfire. They all wanted to have a go themselves afterwards and of course couldn't make the brush do anything except flip over on its back.

They danced about, clapping their hands. 'Show us again, mister! Show us again! *How'd you do that?*'

A couple of older girls trailed him for a while, watching him work, asking where he was from, why they hadn't seen him before. One of them pointed to the other. 'She wants to know are you seeing anybody.'

'God forgive you, I never said that at all. It was you.' To Mark: 'It was her, I swear.' And she stomped off dragging her friend behind her, shouting at her to stop her laughing, it wasn't fucking funny in the slightest.

They didn't bother with a tea break: the yard was closing at twelve for the long weekend. By the time they started making their way back it looked as though the whole of the Shankill had come to a halt.

Big Lad was first out the gates. Mark would have put anything on his dad's Beamer being parked a hundred yards down the road, engine running.

He and Casper decided to walk into town via the Alp.

Large groups of men had congregated outside the bars facing on to the Road. Mark knew the reputation of some of these places. A couple of them had featured by name in the trials of the Shankill Butchers the year before. The details, Mark's mother had said, made the heart shrivel, and nothing in all that he heard or read at the time captured his own feelings better. The taint had seemed to spread out to cover the whole Road. The word was then that a lot more people who drank in those bars knew what had been going on than ever stood before a judge.

Anybody they didn't know or didn't like the look of ran the risk of being pulled inside for a doing.

Whether it was the couple of bottles of beer earlier, though, or the fact that they had a fortnight's work in the surrounding streets under their belts, he walked without fear, as though he had every right to be here. Casper too.

'Have people been giving you money as well?' Casper asked and squinted against the sun, which had taken up its noontime position directly above the city centre. 'It's mad.' Then after a moment, 'This must be what Christmas is like in Australia.'

'Some fucking tree,' Mark said. He meant the bonfire, which had just that moment come into view across half an acre of rubble, with a pope on the top instead of a fairy, and tyres in their hundreds up the sides for decoration. Little satellite fires had already been lit, kids too keyed-up or too young to wait for the main event.

Casper dipped his hand into his shirt's breast pocket and brought out a roll-up, twisted closed at one end. 'Here,' he said and sparked it up, 'have a blast on that.' Mark glanced quickly left and right, back over his shoulder. 'Don't worry, nobody's going to smell a thing with all this smoke around.'

So they passed the little joint backwards and forwards a couple of times and walked the rest of the way into town la-la-la-la-la-la-la-ing Ding Dong Merrily on High.

The pat-down at the Royal Avenue security gates was just about the funniest thing that had ever happened.

Oh, po-faced Belfast! Lighten the fuck up!

'See you Tuesday,' Mark said when they had reached the other end.

'Yeah, see you Tuesday.'

Mark stayed in bed the whole of the Twelfth Day. In *bed* bed. Dennis had agreed to let him have the box room over the weekend. (The books were still lying on the floor where Mark had knocked them over the start of the week before.) He had agreed to strip the sheets and pillowcase too but hadn't bothered his head. Mark was already in the bed when he realised, and by then he wasn't getting out again for anything. There was something a little comforting about it too, that particular smell, neither pleasant nor unpleasant, that was just Dennis. All those nights when they were kids, Dennis calling over to him from his bed, 'You asleep?' then padding across the floor and getting under the blankets with him. Lying there half the night, it felt like, talking and making up stories with the two of them as the heroes, of course. Then their mother coming in, 'Right, you, back into your own bed. And shush, the pair of you! It's nearly ten o'clock.'

He had left the window on the second hole of the latch. He awoke to the sound of flutes not far distant: a band meeting its lodge on the way to the Belfast parade's assembly point at Carlisle Circus. When he awoke again it was close to midday and the sound of the bands was both denser and less distinct – louder and then quieter as the parade route twisted and turned through the city centre and on out towards the Field. His granddad had taken him once when he was very small, though the Field was in a different place then. (Where was Jilly that day? Where was Dennis? Where were his mother and father? Mark didn't remember.) More people than Mark had ever seen. The collarettes the Orangemen wore were gold-fringed Vs on the front of their white shirts. There were huge big tents with sandwiches and buns. A man asked Mark if he would like an ice cream and went away and came back with a rectangular cone. The ice cream was a yellow block, like margarine, starting to melt. Mark let it drop on the grass. His granddad made him pick it up and take every last bit of grass off it, but he was crying so much in the end his granddad snatched it off him and wiped his hands with his big handkerchief, which only seemed to make the stickiness worse. All the rest of that day, that was all he could feel. Sticky, sticky, sticky. His granddad told him he was an ungrateful wee boy and he was never bringing him here again. And he never did. Any time since he had had that sensation, though, using the muscles at the base of his fingers to force two of them apart, Mark was right back there among the marchers, shoes off some of them to rest their aching feet, the preachers and the hucksters, anticipation barely pausing at pleasure before giving way to unpleasantness, disgust.

In the early afternoon he heard Jilly singing, trying to get Danielle over. (Nights when he was on that side of the wall and she on this with Radio Luxembourg on. Whiskey in the Jar, This Town Ain't Big Enough for the Both of Us. Waiting for those bullet sounds.) She must have sat on the bed with the baby eventually, for it was close enough to Mark's own head he could make out every word, every plosive and fricative. Puff the Magic Dragon. He wondered if Jilly would skip the last verse, Puff, outgrown, sadly slipping into his cave, or maybe do what he remembered their own father doing and adding in extra lines about Jackie Paper coming back – 'You didn't think I'd left you, Puff?' – but before he could find out he fell asleep again.

It was five o'clock when he finally came downstairs.

They were all there. Jilly and Danielle, Dennis and his mother.

His father was sitting with the evening paper, pictures on the front of banners and women in Union Jack dresses and hats.

His father raised his head over the top of it, fifteen years more than the man who had given Puff a second chance at happiness. 'We were beginning to wonder if you had died up there,' he said.

'Always the one with the cheery thought,' said Mark and his father, smiling thinly, went back to the paper.

Whoever had been brought in over the weekend had cleared the street corners of the worst of the debris from the bonfires. There were scorch marks still on the roads and up a few of the gable walls (King Billy on one looked like he had stuck his head into the mouth of a cannon). A couple of the telegraph poles on Mark's squad's route were write-offs.

'They have special squads,' Paul said. 'They're the same ones they send in after riots.'

'And car bombs,' said Tony.

Paul nodded. 'Car bombs too.'

'Was it really nuts round here?' Mark asked.

'Tell you the god's honest, I was near asleep on the sofa,' Tony said. 'If it hadn't been for the kids keeping on at me – *Daddy, Daddy, come on, they're starting*, all like that there – I'd have forgotten what night it was. I said to Brenda, can you not take them on your own, but here she was, it's a *family* night get up off there and get on you.' He tidied a pile for Mark to shovel. There was a gospel tract in among it. *Where will you spend* … and nothing more. 'Wasn't bad. Saw Alec with a crowd of wee dolls, acting the gaunch as usual. The fella's nearly twenty-three. Time he started wising up.'

'You'll hear that on the news, right after the announcement about hell freezing over,' Paul said.

When they got round to Tony's house that morning Tony went straight up the stairs. 'What do you think of this?' he said when he had come down. A book: *Dharma Bums.* 'Fighting, drinking, scorning convention, making wild love … Adds up to one hell of a philosophy of life,' said the cover.

It looked like it had been rescued from a bin.

'I went down to Smithfield the other day,' he said. 'Know Floods?' Mark knew of it: bought and sold everything. 'Your man there was going to charge me 15p. I said it has 5/3 printed on the front: 12½p. You can't charge me more than it was to begin with. And here he was, all right then, you can have it for ten.'

He flicked through the pages. A couple of them were coming loose. 'Have you read this one?'

Mark didn't even hesitate. 'No.'

'You should. I mean, a lot of it's what you would expect: hopping on and off trains, getting stoned or plastered and jumping into bed with every woman he meets, but there are some parts, the way it's written, just makes you go …' He let his jaw drop, his eyes widen. 'You call him Ray here instead of Sal. Don't know why he bothers, you can tell it's all him.'

He set the book on the arm of the chair on his way to the kitchen. 'You can have the lend of it if you want when I'm finished.'

'I don't know,' Mark heard himself say. 'I've had a bit of a sickener with Kerouac.'

Tony turned in the doorway.

'Well, it's like you say, it's all him, isn't it?'

Tony shrugged. 'Pretty much.'

He didn't talk about the book again or about any of the other ones he read (he'd finished *Dharma Bums* in two days) on those mornings in between working and eating breakfast and catching a bit of instant sleep before going back out to meet Paul and start sweeping streets again.

They fell into a pattern at the house of Mark taking the dishes out after they had finished eating and washing and putting them away. Over the days he worked out where everything went. It pleased him, when he was done, for it to look as though neither of them had been there at all.

He came back through one day, the week after the Twelfth, to find Tony sitting with his book face down on the arm of the chair and his hands clasped in his lap.

'People saw us sitting here they'd think those fellas don't do any work at all, wouldn't they?'

'Maybe.'

'Oh, they would. I've heard them say it even when you're just leaning on your brush a few moments. *Yous have your money easy.* Think about it, but, what it is we actually do do. Think about the stuff we pick up day and daily. I mean, you've been here, what, just over three weeks? And think of the things you've seen that people have thrown away.'

The things he had seen that people threw away. Cigarette butts, cigarette boxes, cigarette boxes' cellophane wrappers, single matches, books of matches, betting slips (ripped), pools coupons (ditto), the remnants of fish suppers, cabbage stalks, potato peelings, mouldy fruit, crisp packets, Smartie tubes, minus the lids with the

letter telling you who you would marry, fishing tackle –
fishing tangle: *fucking stuff* – fishing bait – don't even ask
– mousetraps, rat traps, with victims, tins of paint (take
it away, Casper … carefully), paint thinners, paintbrushes
hardened to a Tintin lick, solid slabs of chip-pan fat,
pots, kettles, lengths of cable, broken mirrors, armchairs
with busted springs, springs, unravelled cassettes, pages
torn from porn mags, broken records, television aerials,
television sets. ('If it's got to the point where they can't be
left in to be repaired, chances are they are fucked up inside.
Approach with caution: for this were you issued with a
shovel and a brush.' The Gospel according to Pal Paul.)

There was a number in the City Hall you could ring
to have bigger items lifted, but fuck all use that was if you
didn't have a phone and the nearest phone box to you had
had its cashbox ripped out. One day they found a rolled-up
blanket in an entry, which, when they went to lift it, had a
dog's tail sticking out one end. They walked round the other
end and sure enough there was the muzzle, a bit grey, but
not what you would have called old looking. They stood in
a circle around it debating whether abandoning it there in
that way had been a cruelty or a kindness. All depended on
how you interpreted the blanket, was what they concluded.
Might have been its favourite bed. Might have been just the
nearest thing to hand to smother it. They reported it when
they got back to the yard at the end of the day.

'Third bucking dog this week,' Samson said.

'And it's not just around here,' Tony said now, 'it's all
over the city, big fancy avenues and everything. I had a

stint the other year on the lorries, out Stormont direction – those streets are practically mansions from one end to the other – and swear to fuck, some of the stuff you saw in those bins, not even in the bins half the time, lying all around them, as though it didn't matter anyway, it wasn't them was going to be picking it up. I'd do a deal here and now with anybody, I'd do their job for my money and they could have mine for theirs – a hundred pound a week, five hundred, whatever. And do you know what, I bet you there wouldn't be one in a hundred – a thousand – could stick it a week. I bet you.'

'I'll keep my money in my pocket,' Mark said.

'Wise man,' said Tony. He picked up the book again. 'Five more minutes of this and then we'll go.'

Any time Mark asked if he could pay for stuff, Tony was all, ah, sure I'd be getting it anyway or, I need it for the house.

He remembered Tony saying one day how much he loved barmbrack – see toasted? You couldn't beat it – but no one else in the house liked it, which meant he only got it once in a blue moon. There was a place Mark's mother swore by, did the best barmbrack (and oven wheaten) in Belfast, so he got off the bus a couple of stops early one afternoon on his way home and picked one up for the next day's break.

Tony's eyes that morning as he peeled off the Sellotape the woman in the bakery had used to hold the rustly paper in place ... 'Barmbrack?'

'Best in Belfast, supposed to be.'

'Well, I could have an argument with you about that. But, listen, you didn't need to.'

'I know, but I wanted to.'

Tony didn't take the book out this morning, addressed himself instead to the slices on his plate, their yellow paste turned patchy brown beneath the slick of melted butter.

First bite, he closed his eyes. 'It's like being at my granny's.'

He went back for a third and fourth slice. Halfway through the fourth he sat forward suddenly.

'Fuck sake.'

He spat out.

A chunk of tooth showed up greyly among the half-chewed bread and raisins and the little oven-hardened pip he had bitten down on. He put his finger in his mouth and another grey chunk came out stuck to the end of it.

'You'll need to get that seen to.'

'I'll be all right,' Tony said.

The rest of that morning, though, he was walking around with his hand on his jaw. 'Go to the dentist,' Paul said.

Mark and Paul walked back to the yard together at the end of the day.

'There I was thinking I was doing a good thing bringing him the barmbrack.'

'Wait till I tell you, those teeth of his have been at him for years. He could have broken that on a banana. I told him he was better getting the whole lot out and having done with it.'

Mark asked him if he and Tony had been working together long.

'Four or five years, but I know him from before that. Him and my older boy were inside together.' He must have clocked the shock on Mark's face. 'Around the time of Bloody Friday this was.' Mark had been nine. He could still remember the sound of the bombs going off, everywhere at once, it seemed like. Parents running all over the place even in his estate, wanting to know where their children were. 'The dander was up. A whole rake of young ones from here got scooped for rioting down at Unity Flats, ended up being stuck in the cages in Long Kesh with all the hard nuts, which, if you don't mind me saying, was a bit fucking stupid. They were only wee lads. Mind you, of all of them, I'd say Tony was the one able to hold his own in there. Like, he's quiet and all, but see even now if you get him riled?' He shook his head. 'I wouldn't, that's all.'

Of his own son, Paul said the fella had no sense whatsoever. He held out his brush by way of comparison then reached for something even dafter. 'Imagine Alec and then halve that for gumption. I picked him up from the prison gates and put him straight on a boat and told him not to even think about coming back.' He paused. 'Give him his dues, he's took me at my word. I haven't heard a word from him from that day to this.'

The only people in the house when Mark got home were Jilly and Danielle. Danielle had building blocks round her. Jilly had balled tissues. Her eyes were red-rimmed, her nose raw looking.

'Oh, look, Danielle,' she said, 'it's your smelly Uncle Mark.'

He let it go.

'Where is everyone?'

Jilly shrugged. 'Don't ask me.' She pushed a block towards Danielle with her big toe.

'Are you all right?'

'I'm fine.'

'You look like you've been crying.'

Jilly forced a smile that made her look ten times worse. 'Really? Me? What would I possibly have to cry about?' She searched the balled tissues for the least used, blew into it. 'I am nearly twenty-one years old. I am living in the front bedroom of my mum and dad's house with my fifteen-month-old daughter.' Her fifteen-month-old daughter clacked two blocks together. 'Do you think this is what I had in mind for myself when I was growing up?'

He thought he remembered her talking about being an air hostess. Or maybe she just had the Sindy.

'What about when Danielle starts to school?' As the words were coming out he realised he would be nearly twenty-one himself then.

'I could get myself a *wee job*? Is that it?' She shook her head. 'For someone so smart, you know so little.'

She leaned forward, hands on her knees. 'Doesn't he, Danielle? Doesn't he know very little?'

Whether it was the angle she was coming at her from, or the tone of her voice or just the fact that she wasn't crying now, the baby started to laugh. Jilly got right down on the floor with her. 'Doesnthedoesnthedoesnthe.'

Danielle was on her back now, batting away the tickles she wanted more and more of.

Mark carried on out towards the stairs.

'Oh, by the way,' Jilly said, leaning on one elbow, pushing her hair behind her ear, 'some fella called Steve phoned for you. Twice.'

'What did he want?'

'Me, it sounded like, the way he was flirting.'

'I hate to break it to you, he's like that with all girls.'

She leaned forward to blarge her baby's neck, hair falling again across her face. 'Tell him from me he needs to work on it when he's talking to actual women.'

'Did you remember', Steve asked when Mark rang, 'Ricky's birthday?'

The first of the school gang to eighteen.

'I thought that was last week.'

'It was. His ma and da had him away in the Bahamas. He wants us all to get together tonight.'

Mark knew it could end up mental.

'Would we not be better doing it at the weekend?'

'Nah, he's away off again with the grandparents. They have a house in …'

'South of France, I know, he's told me.' Countless times.

The plan was they would meet for pints in the back bar of Robinson's at half six.

'I don't know that I am going to be able to make it for then,' Mark said.

'Well come later,' said Steve, 'or meet us in Cellini's even. It's all on the ma and da.'

Oh, fuck, they were going to Cellini's too. Definitely mental.

The sign over the door said *Ristorante* but most people Mark knew went to Cellini's to drink wine after chucking-out time. Cellini let them do it so that he could get on with his main business of having sex with his waitresses and any of his customers who showed willing. Nobody ever ordered anything but spaghetti bolognese that they smothered with Parmesan cheese, a bowl of which sat at the centre of every table – like the sugar bowl at home – topped up as required from a drum that Cellini himself carried round the restaurant under his arm.

Sheila, a friend of Mark's who used to work there (and had let Cellini have sex with her on her very first shift, 'get it out of the way'), told him that whatever wasn't used at the end of the night was chucked back into the drum. The stuff you were sitting shovelling into your bake while you guzzled your Chianti could have been a month or more old.

Which didn't stop the food tasting better than anything else in Belfast then, even without all that wine.

Mark seriously thought about not bothering his head, about opting out of the whole turning-eighteen thing right at the start. His wasn't until the first week of March. Two-thirds of the ones he hung about with would already have had theirs. Two-thirds of the ones he hung about with all asking him the same question: What are you going to do?

Have a shower. If he was to go out at all he couldn't just get by on a quick wash. He dithered so long his father got in ahead of him for his wash and shave. Then Jilly had to give Danielle her bath.

Seven came and went. Half seven.

He sat, after he showered, on the edge of the bath watching the water run off his feet into the peach-coloured bathmat. It was gone eight o'clock. Another few hours and he'd be tucked up in his bed. Lounger.

He chucked the towel on the floor.

Ah, fuck it.

He could probably still have made it to Robinson's, but he got off the bus in the end a couple of stops before and went for a pint by himself. Needed to get into the right frame of mind. He hadn't seen a single one of his friends since they finished school the month before. The feeling of dislocation was nothing unusual. He had always moved in different summer circles to most of them, more Ballywalter than Bahamas – that was the eleven-plus for you: got you through the door then left you to make the best of it – but a few days back at school or a couple of hours in the bar and all that was erased. Normally.

He ordered a second pint. Took his time over it.

Ten o'clock.

He could fit in another quick one.

He arrived at Cellini's as Ricky and Steve and the rest of them were trying to work out where everyone was going to sit. He couldn't even tell how many of them there were, they were moving about that much – falling about, a few of them – asking other customers, was this seat free, was this one.

'Tighter! Tighter!' Cellini was directing two of the waitresses who were pushing tables together. 'Tighter!' he said again, loving it.

Mark ended up squeezed between a guy called Garry who was a cousin of Ricky's and a wooden room divide. He must have been sitting there ten minutes before Ricky even noticed him.

'How's the binman?' he called down to him from the head of the tight-tight tables.

'I'm not on the bins, I'm road-sweeping.'

'Pardon me.' Ricky had two badges pinned to his lapels: *I AM 1* on the right and *8 Today* on the left. 'How's the *road sweep*?'

It was the first a lot of the people round the table had heard about it.

'You're doing what?'

'Seriously?'

'Your man Casper from Upper Sixth is working there too,' Mark said. He knew this was on a par with him telling Alec on his first day at the yard that he had an aunt living down the road as though it gave him legitimacy.

'*Casper*? The hippy?' That from Steve, who had been wrapped around a girl called Alice since they sat down. 'We could do with some of his blow tonight all right.'

Ricky took a big swallow of wine. 'And how are the nai—'

'Fuck sake!' Janine, sitting on Ricky's right, and possibly going out with him now, slapped the back of his hand.

'What?'

'You were going to say natives.'

'I wasn't. Neighbours. I was going to say neighbours.'

'Sure you were.'

'My ma grew up on the Shankill Road, I'll have you know.'

'Aye, in the manse.'

Ricky shrugged this off. Shrugged it all off.

'Is your sister still back living with you?' Janine asked Mark. They had sat together the entire year in Add Maths, written wee notes on each other's exercise books. *Do you understand a word of this . . . ?!? I like your man's tie today . . . Not.*

'I was speaking to his sister this afternoon,' Steve said. He leaned forward to look at Mark. 'I think she fancied me.'

'So you're still on the camp bed?' Janine said. Camp bed had sounded better than sun lounger when he first told her about it, although he didn't know there was much to choose between them. Janine smiled and he honestly thought she meant it. 'That must be pretty good fun.'

Ricky wasn't finished with the summer job. 'I thought you might have had on your donkey jacket.'

'You have to be there six weeks before you get one.'

'Yeah, Ricky, any fool knows that,' said Steve and rolled his eyes.

'Same for the boots and the overalls,' Mark said. He was starting to feel truculent.

'Be worth it all the same for that, wouldn't it?' said Janine. 'Do the full Dexy's.'

It's worth it anyway, Mark wanted to tell her. Someone else was saying that in Venice they came around your door in the morning on a boat and took your rubbish away, but Ricky drowned them out, beating his fists on the table and chanting, 'Geno! Geno! Geno! Geno!'

Soon the whole lot of them had joined in, stand-up air-horn section and everything (Janine was on trombone). 'Back in '68 in a swea-ea-ty club... Oh, Geno!'

Cellini stopped by the table, laid hands on a couple of lucky lady shoulders, kneading. 'How are all my good friends doing for wine?'

'Could do with more down here,' Mark said, holding up his glass by the base. A load more. Fuck them. Fuck them all.

At one point he counted ten litre-flasks on the table.

It was well past midnight when they downed their last sambuca and staggered out the doors on to the deserted street. Not a prayer, at that hour, of a bus. The other thing Cellini's had going for it, though, was the taxi bunker directly facing, all reinforced doors and a single intercom vent set into the back wall for communicating with the unseen staff. If you were lucky there would be no one else sitting there when you went in who could overhear you tell the intercom where you wanted to go. More than once Mark had preferred to take his chances walking or hailing a car with a dodgy looking taxi sign on its roof to sitting in the waiting room with a crowd of fellas who had a problem with the part of town he lived in.

Tonight was different. Tonight there were so many of his own crowd rammed inside that a couple of other people who stuck their heads round the door thought better of it and struck out again walking. Not fear, you wouldn't have thought – though who knew? drink was drink no matter who it was in – more like simple logistics: a waiting room that packed? Could be an age before there were cars enough to clear it.

And they were not wrong.

'Twenty minutes, there,' was the intercom's most optimistic guess at the arrival of the first one.

'Have we any more drink?' Ricky asked from his position – half lotus – on the waiting-room floor. Somebody had reversed the badges on his lapels, putting sixty-three years on him (*It's all gone by in the blink of an eye*), though even without that he looked haggard.

One of the girls Mark didn't recognise – a friend of Garry's? – had brought the sambuca bottle out of the restaurant. She had done a swap with Cellini, she said, for the knickers she had had on her, though she wouldn't let anybody look to see if she was telling the truth. (Ricky had come out of the lotus and adopted the panting dog.) Maybe later, one of them, she said, if they played their cards right.

Last Mark saw her she was throwing up in the entry next to the bunker, a friend standing beside her, holding back her hair for her, empty bottle on the ground by her wide apart feet.

Steve hung out the window of the taxi taking him and unseen others to New Forge Lane. 'What a fucking night! What a fucking night! Belfaaaaaast!'

Mark could barely remember getting into his own taxi (it dropped someone else off on the way, but who? where?), had no memory at all of getting out.

He was still drunk when he awoke – late, *fuck* – spread-eagled on the sun lounger. His head was busting, his clothes stank, his breath against his hand stank, and as for his farts – he had better hope (memories of his boiled-egg madness) he stayed awake on the bus in case one slipped out while he dozed.

He needed the toilet almost as soon as he was out the door – out the door and running: no time to go back if he wanted to make clocking-on.

'If you don't mind me saying, you look like you should be home in your bed,' said the searcher at the Donegall Place gates. (Where did they all go to the toilet?)

'I don't mind, but I'm fine.'

He wasn't.

Just hold on to the yard.

He got there with a minute to spare and made a beeline for the toilets. Two of the three cubicles were occupied (smoke drifting up bluely from the middle one). The other had an out-of-order sign on the door. He nearly took it down and used the thing anyway.

Why hadn't he just let Samson dock his first hour's pay – mark him down as out for the whole day, if he wanted – and gone back into the house while he still had the chance?

He hung around as long as he could before he heard Paul calling for him to come on, this wagon train was moving out.

A couple of times as they walked down the long street to the Crumlin Road a wave came over him and it was all he could do then to stay on his feet. He told himself he was going to have to find an out-of-the-way entry, but then it came back to him, as vivid as a Polaroid, last night, the girl with sambuca bottle, feet apart, hair held back, puking her guts up. Somebody was standing there right this minute, with a cart and a shovel, looking down at that and taking a deep, deep breath.

He didn't know how, but he would hold on.

By the time it got to ten past eight he was in the coldest of cold sweats. He parked up the cart. At last. Ten more minutes – less – he would be at Tony's.

Tony and Paul were deep in conversation about lead valleys. Paul's were in a terrible state. Tony knew a man, was married to a friend of his sister-in-law's, not hard to pay, if Paul wanted his name. Neither of them seemed to register that it was tea-break time. Paul leaned a shoulder against the entry wall and took out a scrap of paper, checked every pocket before he found a pencil.

'Let's see if I can remember his number,' Tony said. 'Three, two ... No, three, *four* ...'

Mark was standing back flat against the wall.

He would die here. He would definitely die.

Please, please, please, *please*.

'You coming round to mine?' Tony said at last.

Oh halle-fucking-luja!

There was a further excruciating delay while Tony went into the corner shop. Then they ran into the kids on the street, late this morning for their Auntie Sally's, keen, the younger ones, to dance around Mark.

They were close enough that he could see the house. He knew the door would be open.

'Do you mind if I run on ahead?' he asked Tony. 'Just got to nip to the loo.'

'Fire away, I'll be right behind you.'

In the front door, through the sitting room and kitchen in a dozen shuffled steps, out again, into the yard.

He only just made it, sliding the bolt and fumbling at his trouser button, his zip, already squatting, and, oh, the aching, sweet *relief*. He bent forward on the wooden seat sobbing into his knees. A pat, he was thinking, I've shat an actual pat. Even his headache eased.

Luckily he had the napkin from Cellini's in his trouser pocket, a couple of Kleenex too. He was a fucking mess back there. Didn't want to have to be using the whole roll of toilet paper.

He stood to do up his trousers, pulled the chain. It rattled, but nothing happened. He pulled again, harder. A rattle, nothing more. He pulled a third time, two-handed, felt the metal lever strain against the cistern, then just as it seemed as though it hadn't worked – just as he began to loosen his grip – the water came rushing down, spreading out and round, and forced everything, forced itself, clear of the bowl. And then – a burp almost, or a gag – in the next instant the whole lot came back up again. Right, right up. He leapt out of the way as it flowed over the rim, across the floor and under the door, where the sill was worn down, into the yard.

It kept coming.

He pulled the bolt, stumbled out, shouting, 'Tony! Tony!'

He was still out there on the street for all Mark knew. He shouted louder. '*Tony!*'

The back door opened. Tony stood there. The water was an inch deep in his yard. There was a child's ball floating in it, and much else besides.

'Jesus, Tony.' Mark had retreated to a corner of the toilet door sill, next to the jamb, one foot resting on top of the other. 'I'm sorry.'

Tony looked up at him for the first time. His face was purple.

He snatched a wooden pole down from beside the washing line, hooks at both ends of it. For a moment Mark thought Tony meant to break it over his head, or worse. Instead he fished around in the water with it until – *clunk* – he struck something else metal. He yanked. The lid of the grating flipped up and over. He worked the pole into the hole, and worked and worked. At last, the water started to drain away.

They stood looking at one another across the midden of the yard. Tony's shoes were saturated. The napkin from Cellini's had washed up a foot to his right, a dark red blot.

Mark went to apologise again, but Tony got there first. 'Fucking toilet,' he said. He threw the pole down and turned back into the house.

They barely said two words to one another the rest of that day. It came on to rain just after lunch. (At least, Mark thought, it might help clear the yard.) They sheltered for a time under the awning of a bricked-up cinema, either side of Paul, who talked for three, about coming here with his best mate on a double date and the girl Paul was to see taking one look at him and turning and walking back up the road, so rather than sitting there all night listening to those other two courting he took himself off into town, and wasn't it a good thing he did, because as he was queuing up there to get into the Ritz (lovely picture house, the Ritz was, he interrupted his story to say) he got talking to a girl whose date had stood her up.

'And do you know who that was?' A glance at the faces staring out blankly from the left of him and the right. 'Correct. It was Jean. Thirty-eight years married and still going strong.' A few minutes later, 'Looks like that's starting to ease up.' A couple of seconds after that, 'It is, Paul, it's easing up rightly.'

'That creep Steve was looking you again,' Jilly said when Mark got home. 'I said to him, did he not tell you he has work? And here he was, aye, but I thought maybe after the state he was in last night he mightn't have made it today.' She broke off to frown at him. 'You want to watch out for that, you know.'

'Will you stop going on and on about me having a drink now and again? I suppose you never let a drop pass your lips when you were my age?'

'Drunks are born, not made,' she said.

'What does that mean?'

'What it says, some people can handle it and some can't.'

'I think you might need to get out of the house a bit more.'

'There's no might about it.'

Big Lad caught him up just short of the gates the next morning. 'Did you hear? Andy Owens was given his cards yesterday.'

'Which one's Andy Owens?'

'Sandy moustache, big thick glasses.'

'What did he do?'

'I'll give you three guesses.'

'Tea break?'

'In one!'

'You'd think they'd let him off with just a warning.'

'They've been told to crack down.'

Paul said it was nothing at all to worry about. Andy had been caught working behind the counter of a mate's shop in the middle of his shift. He was wearing an overall, for dear sake. It was hardly what you would call a typical case. 'Give it a day or two,' he said, 'I guarantee you, it'll all go back to normal.'

It was, by the standards of recent years, which is to say every year from when Mark was about six or seven, a quiet summer. Bomb scares – bombs themselves – didn't count. Those were just part of the puzzle of your day, like opening the fridge in the morning and finding you had no milk:

So, what'll I do now?

You were supposed to be in such a place at such a time and the buses were all off ... You needed a new pair of football boots and the Athletic Stores was gone ...

So, what'll I do now?

The deaths were what you really listened out for. Since the evening of the first day he started in the yard, three weeks before, not a single person had been killed in the city of Belfast. Then the police shot a boy painting on a wall. A boy just a few months younger than Dennis. Claimed they mistook his paintbrush for a gun.

Opinion in the yard was divided: it was a tragedy all right, but you had to see it from the police's point of view, they had only a split second to react otherwise it could be them lying dead on the Ormeau Road ... Aye, but you had to admit, it looked bad. How could anybody mistake a paintbrush for a gun? What way would you have to be holding it for it to look like a threat? And who hadn't painted on a wall one time or another?

Then again, he was writing *PROVOS* so, you know, reap what you sow.

OK. But sixteen, like. Sixteen.

Tony didn't really join in. He had taken to bringing a book to read while they waited for their shift to start. Once they were out on the road, though, he was a bit more like himself. Not chatty exactly but not avoiding talking either, all the focus on the task at hand.

'Some cat's left a bird under a windowsill there. Robin, I think it's been. You might want to scoop it up before any kids see it.'

As soon as it got to tea break, however, he turned and started walking off on his own. He had a message to do. He'd see them both back here, usual time.

The day after that he said one of the kids was sick. He hoped Mark didn't mind, but he didn't want her passing anything on. 'No, of course, you're just right, I hope she's feeling better soon.' The next day was Saturday. Thank God. Some weeks you needed it more than others.

Mark was actually looking forward to going back in when he woke on Monday morning. He had spent the weekend helping around the house. His father had been talking for ages about putting chipboard down in the roof space, so that they weren't forever hopping from joist to joist when they were up there, afraid of putting a foot wrong and coming through the bedroom ceilings.

The two of them had worked it all out, standing in the landing with the measuring tape and a pencil and paper; the widths they could get through the hatch. They went together to the wood yard in the east of the city and had the boards cut to size, secured them to the roof of the car with ropes passed in one window and out the other, front and back. Mark held on to the ends while his father drove, making sure they stayed taut. Back at the house, he was the one who knelt on the edge of the opening, taking the chipboard as his father passed it up – there was, with each board, a moment when the weight transferred fully from one to the other and his father would be calling up to him, 'Have you got it, have you got it?' And Mark would turn with it, almost at head height, and lay it across the boards at his back. 'Got it,' he'd say, and his father in the end stopped asking.

There was no power up there and even with one extension lead plugged into the other down on the landing, the drill cord wouldn't stretch more than a couple of feet in. He had to make the pilot holes with the bradawl. All sixty-four of them. Then it was the screwdriver and sheer brute force.

When the last screw was in it was past half past eight. His father offered him a tin of beer from under the sink, but Mark said he would sooner have a Coke if there was one there.

He went back up into the roof space later to walk across the boards, gently so as not to wake Danielle, make sure they were all sitting flush.

He heard his father talking to his mother in the bedroom below. 'He's a good worker, I'll say that for him,' his father said. 'Not like that other fella.'

And his mother said, 'Ach, Dennis,' like don't be too hard on him.

Last thing Mark did before he climbed down – one foot on the ledge of the hot press, one on the banister – was to take the bradawl to one of the roof beams, at the point where it met the newly laid floor, and gouge out his name and his father's and the date. Then he swept up after him.

His knees ached, and the heel of his hand where the bradawl and the screwdriver had pressed in, but sure fuck. It was a job well done.

Monday morning, he was just waiting for the invitation to tell somebody – *So how did your weekend go?* He bided his time. He and Tony and Paul did the first couple of streets, they turned into an entry, Mark parked the cart, Tony walked off without another word.

Paul watched him go, shook his head. 'What the fuck did you do on him?' he asked Mark.

His mother had been at him again over the weekend about going and visiting his great-aunt. Even just to say hello. 'If she got to hear you had been working there all this time and hadn't bothered calling in she'd be offended.'

Mark didn't know how she would ever get to hear about it, unless his mother told her herself. And like when had his mother last talked to her? Things had changed now, though, with Tony. He had time on his hands in the mornings and he wasn't going to go back to sitting on his arse in an entry.

Getting to her place meant crossing over the Shankill Road itself, the network of streets that used to connect that side of the road with the Falls Road and, a little further up, Cupar Street and the Springfield. In the memories he had of visiting as a little kid that was always the way his father would have come: Donegall Road, Broadway, Falls, Conway Street, cutting out the traffic of the city centre. They were all just road names then, like the names in any other part of town. Now, though, if they had been mad enough to attempt that route, they would have driven smack into a wall, the peace line.

As Mark approached the wall on foot, from the opposite side, the Shankill side, he was struck by how much more solid it looked than the one next to the yard: more definitive – not just a divide between two lots of neighbours (there was no way that was the word Ricky had started to say), but a divide between the present and the past.

If he hadn't had the recent reminder of the address in his pocket he wouldn't have believed he was in the same place at all. One end of the street was all bricked-up terraces. (He thought dominoes again, only now he thought if you pushed one they would all fall.) The other end, his aunt's end, had already been redeveloped: a cluster – *close* – of single-storey houses in pinky-brown brick, their backs somehow all turned to whatever lay now on the other side of the wall down the street.

A woman in a housecoat was out using a milk bottle to water the flowers in a bright little red wheelbarrow next to her door at the entrance to the close.

She paused, seeing Mark, carried on watering then, inaccurately. He gave her a wave that was not returned.

Mark looked at a couple of the doors. He couldn't work out the way the numbering went. He turned nearly a full circle. The woman was still watching him. He asked her if she knew where Mrs Bell lived.

The woman set the milk bottle in the hallway of her house. 'Are you something to her?'

'Nephew. Grand-nephew.'

The woman pointed into the close. 'Left at the end there, second house. You'll be lucky to catch her in, but. She must be up that road ten times a day.'

And sure enough when Mark knocked at the door of the second house there was no reply. As he was walking back down the short front path though he saw a small woman (too small?) come round the corner with a purse in her hand and a white bakery box tied with string. She stopped stock still in the middle of the street. He thought for a moment she would turn and run.

'What do you want?'

'Aunt Irene, it's me. Mark.' No reaction. 'Margaret's son.'

'Margaret?' she looked at him disbelievingly. 'Our Margaret's not married.'

Mark had seen the wedding photos time without number. Aunt Irene standing well to the fore in the group shots – in a royal blue, fur-trimmed coat – taller, definitely, than the woman in front of him, less troubled looking, but Aunt Irene all the same.

The woman who had been watering her plants came and stood at the corner. 'Is everything all right there, Irene?'

Aunt Irene tilted her head. 'You *look* a wee bit like her,' she said to Mark, and, over her shoulder, to the woman at the corner, 'Quit your fussing, Maudie, I'm fine.'

She opened her purse and took out her key as she pushed past him up the path.

'Come on in then if you're coming.'

He stepped into the hall and closed the door. The place still smelled of new plaster. New plaster and ... what *was* that? Emulsion? Whatever it was, after less than a minute he was wishing he could open a window.

Aunt Irene was in the kitchen, making tea, he guessed. She hadn't said to follow. He sat. He thought he remembered the chair, the little wooden ledge at the end of the arms.

'Can I give you a hand with anything?' he called, but she didn't answer. The kettle whistled. When she came back in a minute or two later she still had her coat on. She had a saucer and cup in one hand and plate in the other with a cream doughnut on it. She sat down in the armchair facing Mark's and balanced the saucer on the ledge then started to eat. 'I only bought one doughnut,' she said.

'That's all right, I'm not that long after my breakfast.'

She took a second bite out of the doughnut, chewed for a while then started to cry, full-on tears. For one terrifying moment Mark saw Danielle in her, her in Danielle. 'I can't believe our Margaret getting married and not telling me.'

Her elbow, shaking, knocked the saucer. Mark jumped up and righted the cup before it had a chance to topple. He took it and the half-eaten doughnut from her into the kitchen.

Jesus Christ, the kitchen. That was what he had smelled: bakery boxes wherever he looked. On the cooker, the draining board, on the chairs as well as the table. There was one sitting right in the middle of the floor, the bottom half turned from white to yellow. Something told him to give it a wide berth.

He pushed up the lids of one or two of the others on his way to the back door. Was sorry he had bothered.

He black-bagged as much as he could and put it next to the bin in the back yard.

'What day are your bins lifted?' he asked.

She shook her head.

'All right, Auntie Irene, I'm going to go now, but I'll come back tomorrow. Will you listen out for me? And remember, it's Mark.'

'Mark,' Aunt Irene said.

'That's right.'

On his way out of the close he knocked on the neighbour's door. 'I'm sorry,' he said when she answered, 'I didn't know what you meant about her going up the road all the time.'

'We all do what we can to help,' the neighbour said, 'but she's very private-getting. You can't just barge in without being let. She needs family.'

'I can see that,' said Mark.

He must have walked half the length of the road looking for a phone box that was working. In the end he went into a bookies that was just opening and asked to use theirs. 'It's an emergency,' he said.

His mother when she heard his voice thought it was even worse of a one.

'Is it your father?'

'Dad's fine, it's Aunt Irene.' He told her the whole story. 'We'll have to do something.'

'I don't think it's our place. She has children of her own, grandchildren.'

'Well we'll have to speak to them. The cream in some of those buns, Mum, it was black.'

He set 10p on the counter when he had finished, but the bookies' clerk pushed it right back. 'I'd like to think anybody'd do the same for me.'

Outside again, waiting to cross the road, he saw a bin lorry make a left up the side of a shop with a faded *Closing Down Sale* sign in the window. He chased up after it and caught it just as the crew were slinging the emptied bins on to the footpath for their owners to collect.

Mark reached up and tapped on the driver's door. A face appeared, a spectacular quiff above it. The window was wound down and an arm came out to rest on the sill: cap-sleeved T-shirt, *Sha Na Na* tattooed just below his shoulder.

Complaint was clearly anticipated.

Mark explained who he was, where he worked.

'Listen,' he said, 'I know it's probably not your day for it, but there's a wee woman down the road there, she's on her own, I think she's maybe a bit confused. She has a couple of bags sitting in her yard need lifted.'

The driver asked him the address, then called it out again to the men who had just jumped back up into the cab beside him.

He angled his hand down for Mark to shake.

'Consider it done,' he said.

Mark was dead beat by the time he got back to the entry and wouldn't you know it the second he did the others showed up and that was him back out on the road, working. Silently for the most part.

It was turning into a really muggy day. Even Paul was in bad form. Every street they went down, every entry they looked along had something in it to annoy them further.

'I think there's people come here specially to dump their stuff. I mean who around here uses ...' Paul turned over a bucket-sized tub, oozing gunk '... fucking *horse saddle polish*?' He shaped to kick it then thought better of it, better or himself. 'They probably look at the place and think sure it's falling to pieces already, what's another car boot full of shit going to matter, and who even gives a fuck anyway?'

Somewhere in the middle of the afternoon they were passing one entry they had swept about half an hour earlier when Mark, bringing up the rear, happened to notice a TV set lying face down between two back gates. It looked as though someone – there was no telling from which house – had just bucked the thing over the yard wall. They had probably waited until they had seen the cart go past the last time.

'Bad bastards,' Mark said and didn't care who heard him. He let go the handle of the cart and stomped off back down the alley. He reached over the top of the TV to turn it the right way up and at the same moment as he heard Paul call out, 'Not like that!' saw the middle finger of his glove flip back towards him already filling with blood. It was a second or two before he realised what had happened, before he felt the actual pain ... *the fucking pain*!

He staggered back, trying with his other hand to rip the glove off. He was distantly aware of boots thudding on the ground behind him.

'Leave it on! Leave it on,' Tony was shouting and the next moment was beside him. 'Here, fold that flap over – I'll do it – hold your hand up – up more – right, now don't move it.'

Paul had caught up now too. 'Did you not know, you should never go to lift a TV like that until you've checked the screen's not broken: turn it with your shovel.'

'I don't think he needs to hear that now, Paul,' said Tony.

Blood was coursing over Mark's wrist and down his shirtsleeve. He felt as though his entire upper body was emptying.

'He's completely white,' Paul said.

'We're going to have to get you to the Mater,' said Tony. He went over to the cart and searched around in it till he found a plastic bag – *Stewarts Wine Barrel* – and placed it over Mark's injured hand, tying the loop handles in a tight bow at his wrist.

'How does that feel?'

'Sore.'

'Well, it will be,' said Paul.

'Thank you, doctor,' Tony said.

He led Mark through side streets and entries, his right hand cupped under Mark's elbow to help keep his arm aloft, until they were in a passage up the side of the courthouse, rolls of barbed wire overhanging, a decade's worth of windblown plastic snagged there, flapping.

'Nearly there,' said Tony, and even as he did they were coming out on to the lower part of the Crumlin Road. The Mater Infirmorum Hospital was on the far side of the road, to the right of the jail.

Tony didn't bother with a pedestrian crossing, but marched him right out into the traffic. He shouted at a couple of drivers who sounded their horns, 'Are yous fucking blind?' and raised the arm higher still.

Into A&E and right up to the reception desk. 'This fella's hand's hurt bad,' he said. There was blood on the counter just from his own hand, where it had been supporting Mark's elbow.

He went back to the counter three times more before a doctor with hair in a ponytail pulled back the curtain of a cubicle and called Mark's name.

'You're all right where you are,' she said to Tony who had started to follow. 'I can look after him from here.'

'Don't forget to tell her it was a TV done it,' Tony called, then to the rest of the room, it sounded to Mark, as the curtain was pulled behind him, 'You should never go to lift one until you've checked the screen's not broken.'

The doctor sat Mark on the edge of a metal bed and unbuttoned his shirt, pushing it down below the shoulder – 'I'll give you this,' she said, and did, a sudden fleeting jolt, almost before he was aware that she had a syringe in her hand, 'for the pain.'

She started trying to untie the handles of the plastic bag. 'Your friend's done a pretty good job.' She reached for scissors. The palm of the glove underneath was saturated, deep crimson, but four of the five fingers were almost untouched. The doctor put her hand over her mouth, leaned back against the trolley with all her instruments on it. 'I'm sorry, I don't mean to laugh, but like ...' she mirrored his hand with her own and he saw it then too. The Red Hand of Ulster become the Red Finger.

'Commit this to memory,' she said, then began to cut the glove away, putting herself between him and it. After a minute she had to call in a nurse to assist.

Even with the injection the pain went up another couple of notches as between them they peeled the material back.

'The good news is the pad of your stitched finger isn't *completely* detached. Six or seven stitches ought to do it.' She looked again. 'Eight. Are you squeamish? Now might be the time to face the wall.'

While the doctor got to work on the stitches the nurse went out and came back in with a clipboard and pen and took down his details. The doctor stopped, black thread poised. 'Ah, I see. Summer job. Where are you, Queen's, Coleraine?'

'I'm still at school, just going into my A-level year.'

'A levels!'

He couldn't tell if she was only doing that to flatter him, if she and the nurse were smiling over his head.

'Are you going to tell me too you're right-handed?' she said now.

'I am.'

'That figures. Show me what way you hold your pen.'

The injured finger – he had to show her with the other hand – was the one he normally rested the shaft on.

'You want to make sure that heals properly before you're back to school,' she said. 'I remember my own A-level year. All I seemed to do was write, write, write.' She cut the thread and showed him the stitched finger, swollen to several times its normal size. A bald man after a ten-day bender, florid complexion, grin running wonkily from ear to ear. The nurse helped her apply a bandage, then a fingerstall. Then – the finishing touch – the doctor asked him to lean forward and slipped something over his head. 'Keep this sling on for me the next few days. Any pressure at all and you could burst those stitches.'

Then she said, 'Have you ever had a tetanus?' Mark didn't think he had. 'In that case I'm going to have to ask you to take down your trousers.'

He limped out.

Tony was still out in the waiting area. It was already after knocking-off time.

He knew without asking: 'You had to drop the bags for them then … bend over?'

'You shouldn't have waited.'

'Just wanted to make sure everything was all right.'

He stayed with him at the bus stop too.

'Seriously, you should head on home,' Mark said, 'I'll be OK.'

'"Practise charity without holding in mind any conceptions of charity for charity after all is just a word." That's in *Dharma Bums*,' Tony said and then laughed.

'You're a mate, for fuck sake, you don't just leave a mate when he needs help.'

A bus arrived. Tony stood at the foot of the steps. 'Don't be embarrassed taking one of the Old People's seats. You're hurt. I'll tell Samson not to expect you in the next day or two.'

Mark found an empty seat two back from the Old People's. Someone had written *Kill All Huns* on the window in red marker. Someone else had tried to rub it off. Mark watched through the smudges as Tony – fellow Hun – crossed over the road and up the side of courthouse.

His own doctor when he went to see him next morning gave him a sick line to the start of the following week. 'No sense being silly about this, it's only a summer job.'

'I'm supposed to be saving.'

'As long as you've a line they have to pay you.'

He walked back up home, past the swing park full of kids. Some lads were having a kickabout on the all-weather football pitch. Nobody he recognised though he stopped to watch a while. Kick, rush; kick, rush. A ginger-haired fella put his foot on the ball eventually. 'Want us to pick you on? Russell there has to go in ten minutes.'

'Fifteen,' Russell said.

Mark raised the sling as far as he could. 'I'm not really able.'

The ginger-haired fella shrugged. 'Sure that doesn't matter. Nev's brother done nets one time when he was on crutches.' It didn't make any difference. Twenty more minutes of kick and rush passed. No sign of Russell leaving. That was fine. This is my holiday, he thought, as he walked away: now to Monday.

By half past eleven he was bored out of his skull, wondering what they were up to at work.

He didn't realise until he went up to the box room just after lunch that Dennis was still in bed.

'I thought you'd be away to Lisburn.'

'Not ,the day. Shut the door there when you're going out.'

He didn't go to Lisburn the next day either. Barely left his room in fact. Mark went up to him to tell him his dinner was ready. He was sitting on the bed, writing on his jeans.

'Are you all right?'

'Yeah.'

'You don't look it.'

'I said I am.'

'Come on down, well.'

He was at the door when Dennis suddenly said. 'She chucked me. Been seeing this other fella. Some fucker lives round her way, drives a car and all.'

For a moment Mark nearly felt better, but then he saw his brother was crying. 'Ah, fuck, that's wick,' he said.

'I know. It's her birthday next week, I already had her present.'

He pulled something out from under the bed. It was hard to know what exactly. Pink mainly. It had one purple ear and one white, only they weren't really ears either, they were floppy hearts. It had purple cheeks too and for a tail a pink and white pom-pom on a string.

Julie Warner would never know it, but she had had a very lucky escape.

'What are we having?' Dennis said.

'I think it's vegetable roll.'

He held the door so that Dennis could smell it.

'I'll go and wash my hands … And, here, at least when I go back to school I can tell them I'm not a virgin anymore.'

The next morning, though, the gloom had descended on him again, on them both.

Their mother told Mark while he was sitting having breakfast that Aunt Irene had gone into hospital while they tried to find space in a home.

'Could one of the family not have taken her?'

'They're all away. Besides, she's just too far gone. It's a good job you went round when you did.'

Try as he might, though, Mark couldn't help thinking he had turned the old woman in.

Jilly came into the living room where Mark and Dennis were watching *Why Don't You?* (the English schools were off at last).

'Would you do me a big favour, Dennis? Would you look after Danielle for me for an hour? I'll feed her and change her and everything beforehand. You'll not need to do anything, just take her out a walk. She'll probably fall asleep before you're halfway up the street.'

Dennis said, 'There's no way I'm wheeling a pram around the estate.'

'It's not a pram, it's a pushchair.'

'Same difference, I'm not doing it. What are you asking me for anyway?'

'She can hardly ask me,' Mark said, but Jilly was already looking at him.

'I've pushed it some days with one hand when I've been carrying a full bag of shopping in the other. It mightn't even be for as much as an hour.'

'You're a dick sometimes,' he said to Dennis when she had gone.

'Yeah, well, I'd rather be a dick than a pushover.'

Jilly came back downstairs with a dress on and her hair and make-up done. Mark's first thought was that the Scottish boyfriend was coming for her.

'What are you doing all dolled up?' Dennis asked.

'I've an interview.'

She had Danielle in a dress too.

'Uncle Mark's coming with us a walk,' she said and Danielle looked at him doubtfully.

The interview was with a draughtsman's practice, which had just moved into a big old house about half a mile down the road into town. Mark remembered playing around there when there were people living in it. Mansion they called it. Then haunted mansion when it fell empty. The driveway was still scary looking: overhanging branches, puddles in the gravel no matter what the season.

As they drew close to the front gates, Jilly peeked round the hood of the pushchair. She held up her forefinger and thumb to Mark, narrowing the space between them to indicate Danielle's closing eyelids. Then she stepped to the side letting Mark take the pushchair handle. She tiptoed up the gravel and out of sight behind an overgrown rhododendron. Danielle didn't even notice she was gone.

In nearly every car that passed him, though, a head turned. The sling obviously transformed his pushing the buggy into an act of near heroism. He decided to stick to the main road. Fifteen minutes down the way, fifteen minutes back up.

Danielle didn't stir until he was almost level with the draughtsman's driveway again. She turned in the seat, raising herself and trying to see behind her. He knew she sensed something was different. There was a catch in her breath.

'It's all right, it's all right,' he said and then saw Jilly up ahead, 'Look who it is, see?' and the cry turned into a breathless laugh. 'Mummy!'

Jilly dropped to her knees and undid the straps, stood up again, bouncing Danielle on her hip.

'They offered me it then and there. Two mornings a week, making the teas and filing.'

She stopped bouncing the baby. 'I know what you're going to say,' she said to Mark. 'I did get a wee job after all.' Mark tried to remember if he had ever used the words, but his sister had already moved on. 'I'll have to find a childminder. Probably cost me as much as I'm making, but hey-ho.' He hadn't seen her like this since she came home. 'You might have to stay on the lounger a wee while yet. I'm sorry.'

'Maybe we'll get a proper ladder into the roof space before the end of the summer, or even stairs.'

When he showed up at the bus stop on Monday morning, the people in the queue turned to look at him. He honestly thought that they had erased him from their memories while he had been off.

He had to call in at the hospital to have his finger looked at. The same doctor as last time, though she seemed to have no memory either of having seen him before, reading aloud from the notes on the clipboard the nurse had handed her. 'Lifting a broken TV in a back entry.' Her eyebrows went up. She examined the wound, holding his hand. 'You can lose the sling, but you're still going to have to take it very easy.'

She handed the clipboard back. 'Sorry,' she said. 'We're pretty stretched in here. It took me a minute before I could put a face to it, but I haven't forgotten the red finger.'

He couldn't shovel, just pull down the handle of the electric cart left-handed. Samson had to put Casper on the squad to help with the shovelling.

They didn't go back to Tony's at tea break. Not that Tony asked. He probably thought that Mark and Casper together would be able to put the time in rightly.

Mark was conscious all week of Samson's eyes on him, conscious of him muttering that this was never going to do, never going to do at all.

'Just keep the head down and get on with it,' Paul said. 'That's all you can do.'

He managed to keep the head down until lunchtime Thursday. Payday. He was practically the last one in the queue. 'Young Mark! Close the door over there, would you?' Samson tapped the edge of the buff envelope on the tabletop. It looked thicker than usual. 'I'm sorry about your hand and everything, but let's be honest you're not much use to me like this, are you?' Mark went to answer, but Samson shook his head: it wasn't really a question. 'We'll call tomorrow your last day.' He held out the envelope. 'That has your lying week in it too, and an extra couple of notes forby. Call it a wee bonus.'

'Are you sure bonus is what you mean?' Mark should have said but didn't. Samson must have read the question into his silence anyway. He folded his hands on the table, pressing the meat of his thumbs together, what there was of it. 'I saw you,' he said, 'the day you hurt your hand, coming out of a bookies out on the road. At half ten in the bucking morning? I could have turned you off then and there. I could have written a report to your school. I still could. Do we understand each other?'

Mark nodded. Picked up the envelope and put it in his pocket.

He was almost out the door when he turned. 'What about my donkey jacket?'

Samson sat back. 'How many weeks is this you've done?'

'Five.'

'Close, but rules are rules. Come back next summer. I'll see you're top of the list. You weren't the worst we've had.'

The word had spread around the yard that he was going even before he was out of the office. Samson didn't ask you to close the door over for nothing. 'I wouldn't bother my head coming in tomorrow,' Benny said – the most Benny had ever said. 'They've paid you your wages, they're hardly likely to come round your house looking one day's worth back.'

'That means you've only today,' Alec said, rubbing his hands, 'to buy us all a drink. That's the rule, isn't it?' He looked to the others for support. He may have winked. 'The man that's going buys the drinks.'

'Never listen to him,' said Paul.

Mark had already thumbed through the notes in his pay packet: last week's, the lying week and an extra … twenty quid. 'Sure, I'll buy the drinks,' he said.

Fifteen of them in total filed into the bar. Mark glanced back as he rested his arm on the counter and saw Tony bringing up the rear.

'What are yous all having?'

'Doubles all round!' someone called, then said, Ah, no, all right then, mine's a pint. Paul and a few of the older men wouldn't even let him buy them that much.

'A half will do me …'

'And me.'

Alec had already launched into the story of Mark's first morning at the yard, as if none of the rest of them had been there, almost as though Mark hadn't been.

'Here he was lifting the handles of the cart' – standing up from the table to demonstrate – 'and here the cart was'

– arms weaving this way and that – 'all over the fucking shop, until *bang!* he smacks it into the side of one of the other carts, shovel and all flying every fucking where! And Samson' – he shrank himself to fit – 'he was bawling his baldy wee head off at him, *If you're not able for this bucking job there's hunderds more are. Hunderds!* Swear to fuck, he must have lifted about two foot off the ground, he was shouting that hard.'

Tony shook his head, but he was smiling too, sort of: like typical Alec to be hogging the limelight, but fair play for a story well told.

Mark was barely halfway down his first pint when Paul set him up another. 'Me and a couple of others have organised a float,' he said. 'I don't want to see you put your hand in your pocket again.' He lost track of how many pints were set in front of him after that. People came and went and came back again as the afternoon wore on and tipped into evening. Tony was there and then wasn't there and somebody did the under-the-thumb sign and Mark was thinking that was a bit shit, he could at least have said I'll see you then, or have a good rest of your life or whatever.

At some point he got up and went out to the toilets and when he came back in there Tony was, sitting, as fresh looking as if he had just woken up from a mid-morning kip.

'I had to go home and stick my head in a sink full of water,' he said. 'Some Beat I'd have been … Do you think you'll go away?'

'I don't know,' Mark said. 'Bristol's supposed to be good. Depends what sort of grant I get. I haven't saved a whole load.'

'I'd go if I was you. This place is never going to change. Anyway, students have more time on their hands than even we do. Pick up a brush, earn yourself a few bob, be the same shit there as here, but it'd be worth being knackered if it meant not having to stay at home.'

Sometime after that Mark looked and he was gone again.

Of the fifteen who had come in there were only five left now, including him. He had about an inch of a pint left and a full one next to it. He pushed away the nearly empty and took a swallow from the full, contemplated a second, but no, that was it. He set it back.

'I'm done,' he said.

As he was getting, a little unsteadily, to his feet, Alec got up too and took off his donkey jacket.

'Here, this is for you.'

'Ah, no,' Mark said, 'I couldn't.'

'Stick it on you, fuck sake. I'll tell Samson it got fucking nicked. Couple of big fuckers with knives. That right, Brainiac? You'll back me up.'

'Looked more like machetes to me,' Casper said.

'Right!' Alec draped an arm about Casper's shoulder. 'Machetes!'

They were walking up the aisle of the bus, Mark a couple of paces ahead when Casper suddenly reached out and clapped him on the shoulders. 'Fuck me, I'm only seeing it now.' He scored a finger across the back of the donkey jacket. 'BCC. That's what I need to get into Loughborough: a B and two Cs. Come on, that has to be some sort of an omen.'

*

It was a couple of months into the new millennium and Mark was up in court for drink-driving. Third offence. The judge left him in no doubt he was lucky to be escaping with a £500 fine and a two-year ban. Only the assurances of his AA mentor that he was taking his drinking in hand saved him from worse. As he was leaving the hearing he saw a face he dimly recognised coming towards him, a smile forming. It took him a moment to put a name to it. A nickname: Big Lad.

'Mark, isn't it?' he said. There was grey now, and plenty of it, in among the black visible beneath the horsehair wig. He swapped the briefs he was carrying from the right arm to the left to shake hands. 'Must be … what – twenty years?'

'Must be.'

'Do you ever see anything of …?' His fingers fluttered, reaching for the name.

Mark handed it to him. 'Casper? He died – drowned his first week of university, swimming in some lake.'

'Ah, frig, I'm sorry.' Big Lad shook his head. Allowed a respectful moment to elapse. Then, in the spirit of life goes on, 'Those fellas used to give him some him some stick, all the same. What am I saying, give *him*? Give us all some stick.' He leaned closer, made a play of speaking past the back of his hand. 'Can you imagine if they'd known I was a Taig?'

Mark's expression must have said he didn't know it either.

Big Lad laughed and smacked his thigh. 'Why do you think I never minded all that Big Lad crap? That's all I was, right from the start. Didn't occur to a single one of them to ask any more.'

A door opened along the corridor and a man in a pinstriped suit searched the passing faces, then caught Big Lad's eye and beckoned with a crooked finger.

'I'd better get on here,' he said. 'I never even got asking what you're at. Are you doing OK?'

'Yeah ... OK.'

'That's good, that's good.' He was a few steps up the corridor when he turned back. 'Here, do you remember a fella called Tony? Sort of skinhead? I bumped into him here, let's see, last year.'

Mark's heart contracted, almost as much as when the judge just now had dangled the word 'custodial' before opting for the ban and fine. He wasn't sure he was ready to hear what had brought Tony's life and Big Lad's back into alignment.

'His daughter was called to the bar,' Big Lad said.

Fla-fla? Mark tried to do the maths. He remembered a girl standing on the stairs in open-toed sandals and socks. Early thirties now, would be. Yes.

'He's got a bit beefier, like the rest of us,' said Big Lad, who had not got the least bit beefier, 'but you would still know him: same haircut and everything.'

'Did he say what he was up to?'

Big Lad shrugged. 'Same as ever, though he was saying it's all changed – the carts and everything. Most of the time now he says he's out there on his own. Not that he was complaining. He asked after you. I told him I hadn't clapped eyes on you since. And now look.'

He waved over his head as he carried on his way. 'Don't for goodness sake let it be another twenty years.'

Outside, Mark crossed the road to the bus stop in front of the Waterfront Hall, looking back at the law courts and the people coming and going across its wall-sized post-ceasefire windows. A perpetual strip cartoon of strife and woe.

He couldn't account for anything that had happened in the last twenty years. 'Time,' he said out loud and the woman with the baby sitting next to him shifted a couple of inches further up the red vinyl bench. He said it again, under his breath. 'Bucking time.'

Last Summer of the Shangri-Las

A s BEST AS I AM able to reassemble it this is the story
of what happened the summer I was sixteen. What
happened to me I mean and the handful of people whose
paths crossed mine. My mother had phoned my Aunt
Heather in New York halfway through the first week of
the holidays. I need you to take him for a while. He's
going to end up dead if he stays here. My aunt said gee
(like she had been saying it all her life) I don't know. I
mean I know things are bad over there but this is New
York you know? My mother said you don't understand. If
he stays here any longer I'm going to strangle him myself.
I had been refusing to wear clothes around the house – I
was standing at the top of the stairs as she talked hand to
one side of her head trying not to see – I would be the first
to say she wasn't having an easy time of it. *Even a towel for
Christ sake – a facecloth!*

My aunt had a couple of simple rules: (1) stay out of
Times Square after 6 and don't go there much before 5.59
and (2) let there be so much as a single pubic hair on display
and you are on the next flight back to your own funeral.

She told me I was to call her Hedda here. That was
part of what New York was all about. So I said OK call me
Gem. Gem? Gem. All right then: Gem.

The lights went out across the city the night I got
there. Now look what you went and did Hedda said like
I had brought the blight with me. Between strikes and

bombs and three-day weeks the lights had been off as often as they had been on while I was growing up.

She gave me the tour of the apartment by the light of a two-foot candle: you're on the sofa here I'm in the bedroom there that's the kitchen this is the bathroom roach spray behind the sink.

It was hot that summer in New York (no suggestion I'd brought that). Hot enough for it to be front-page news any time there wasn't a blackout or a serial killing to report. Some guy with a gun and a thing about couples in cars. For the first few days after the power came back I was fit for nothing but lying on the sofa that I slept on watching TV – who knew there was so much TV to see? – and wondering if I would know a cockroach if I saw one. (I did and I did. Straight off.)

Hedda worked in a deli: West 74th Street she told me as though it meant something more to me than subtract thirty-seven from where I lay all day watching TV. She was gone in the morning before I was awake. Don't ask me how I slept through it. There was only one small spot in the bathroom clear of debris when I eventually went in there: the seat of the explosion. Tubs and tubes brushes of all shapes and sizes – balled tissues cotton wool bruised deep reds and blues – flung to the furthest extremities of the room.

First thing she did every night when she got home was stick a record on tie a scarf in her hair and put everything back where it had been before the bomb of her went off ten hours earlier.

I watched that like it was a show too on one of those channels whose studios looked like the insides of the presenters' own houses. Watched and learned. The start of the second week she came home and I had already tidied and put away for her. She checked the baskets and cabinets. Tried lids to make sure they were on right. Her eyebrows twitched then bunched up then settled finally one a little higher than the other. I think maybe I'll keep you after all. But still (her eyebrows suddenly arrows) no pubes.

She liked the Jackson 5 when she was cleaning up or when she was cooking – though most of what we ate came in cartons from the deli: twenty minutes at 400°F let rest for five – she liked Stevie Wonder: Superstition Misstra Know-it-all. Give a hand to the man yeah she would sing and her own hand would shoot into the air index finger pointing. Give a hand to the man that's got the plan … When she was sitting at night though her balloon glass half filled with red wine it was Dusty Springfield she kept going back to. I say *back*. It was all new to me. I had been listening to nothing but Radio 3 since I was old enough to find it on the dial. That was another thing drove my mother mad. I don't want a bloody education. I just want something I can sing along to!

Hedda was my mother's younger sister by seven years. She had already been married once – *less than a year older than you are now: think about that* – which was how come she was in New York to begin with. She had got a job the summer she left school waitressing in this fancy hotel – lodge they called it – in the Adirondacks. (The word seemed made of Stickle Bricks the way she said it. Stickle Bricks and red wine.) This guy came in every lunchtime without fail always a big crowd around him always a lot of women. Oh he was good looking and he knew it but sometimes you know Gem that is attractive too. You want him to notice you *not* falling for him. You go right out of your way in fact. And then he does notice and even while you're thinking that will show him you are sort of flattered and the next thing you really are falling and well – draining her glass finally – people can say what they like that I got the Green Card and the nice apartment but do you know what? He got the better end of the deal – reaching for the wine again – you better believe he did. He got me for all those years when I should have been off with people my own age having a bit of fun.

And all the while Dusty was chiding don't tell me what to say and don't tell me what to do or she was asking that the eyes that had watched her man walk away be coloured grey and not a few nights an unwiped tear or two brimmed over from Hedda's own eyes as she emptied the last of the wine into her glass and the clock hands squeezed the little that was left of the day between them: sometimes snuffed it out completely. Then – boom! – it was morning and she was off again before my eyes were even open.

Maybe those regular doses of Dusty were what kept her antennae so finely tuned to heartache and its purveyors. Maybe that was why she and she alone of the deli staff reacted the day the young woman in jeans and a halterneck top (same as fifty young women before her in the other staff's defence) walked up to the counter and ordered a slice to go.

Hedda flung open the door that evening hair sticking to her forehead from the race to get home in headline-making heat and without taking her bag off her shoulder went over to the cabinet where the record player lived.

This girl came in today. (She had the door of the record rack open and was tilting LPs back by the top left-hand corner, letting them drop again.) I'd seen her across the street talking to two other girls and a blond-haired guy. I knew her right away. I said to Rena I got this. Like Rena could care less. I looked at her as she was searching in her purse for her two quarters. I wasn't going to say it but then I thought what the heck: you're not who I think you are are you? Here she was: depends who you think I am – but not in a snarky way – I mean she smiled and then she dropped the quarters into my hand and then out she strolled again eating her slice.

She tilted an LP – maybe the tenth she had tried – and pulled it out. *Golden Hits of The Shangri-Las*. She pointed. There she's there. Dark brown hair stopping short of two enormous hoops of earrings eyes narrowed in a smile head angled to the left, right arm swinging almost out of the frame. She wore a white vest top turquoise slacks and lime green boots that completed a set with the lime green slacks and pink boots on the honey-haired girl next to her – the pink and turquoise combination on the girl – hair hanging down across one eye – next to her again.

Hedda traced the outline of the first girl's face with her index finger. Can you imagine? I mean I've seen people now and then off the TV – Archie Bunker's wife what's this you call her … I saw her … she was coming out of Macy's side door one day as I was going in – but like this was … she was standing right in front of me talking to me the way I'm talking to you buying a slice of cheese pizza.

I asked her about the other two – with the green slacks and the pink and – now that I looked at them again – with not just the hair but the eyes nose and mouth of sisters. Was that them did she think across the road with the blond guy? Hedda said she couldn't say for sure. If it was them they looked pretty different now. One of them was wearing glasses: huge purply lenses.

Might have been two other girls entirely. But not the girl she sold the pizza to. She was who she was. She'd stake her life on it.

The record rasped against cardboard as she slid it out. No inner sleeve.

I flipped the cover over where she had dropped it on the rug. Read a bit. It says here on the back there were four of them. Betty Weiss and her sister Mary, Marge and Mary Ann Ganser.

Hedda paused record pinched between forefinger and thumb taking the weight of itself. I think Betty and Mary were the fair-haired ones. That must have been a Ganser then.

I wonder why there are only three of them on the front?

Hedda shrugged. Maybe they just ran out of slacks-and-boot combinations.

There was already a record on the record player. You could buy record players then that were specially designed to hold multiple records – singles LPs: singles and LPs together even. This wasn't one of them. Hedda set the *Golden Hits* down on top regardless. It took her three goes to land the needle which was two fewer than it usually took her. It popped and jumped all the way through the first song and on into the second where it skated a while.

How long have you had this?

Donkeys.

She lifted the arm up with a finger under the cartridge head blew a pea-size ball of fluff off the needle and dropped it down at the third song. More or less. A rising violin note bringing the song before to a close then a train whistle – piano rolling way down in the bass notes, shuffle drums overlaid with tambourine. Four voices wrapping around one another – baby baby please believe me I would never never do anything to hurt you …

And then the most plangent of the voices – of all the voices I had ever heard – broke free telling us – or telling baby – all about a letter she had got the day before from this guy she used to love – in Kansas City must have been because that's where the train whose whistle we kept hearing was coming from and nothing she could do could make it turn around – there was that rolling piano again only now it wasn't just a train it was bringing but trouble too – and she was telling baby he wasn't to worry she was going to the station to meet the train – ten after two – but she was going to be back in the time it took to break a heart – I felt the words like a stab in my own – she had to break the guy's heart. She had to show him the ring on her finger; the ring she hadn't been able to write before now to tell him about. Then the other three voices were back supporting her again – more gang of friends than group: here comes the train here comes the train here comes the tray-ay-ain … And if I had been Baby listening to its approach I would not have been taking it for granted I was ever going to see her again.

I looked at Hedda when it was over. She was sitting back on her heels against the wall hair all pushed up bag still on her shoulder a cigarette hanging unlit from her lips.

I don't think I want to listen to anyone else again ever I said.

She spun the wheel of her lighter a couple of times before she got a flame then allowed it to go out again. I should have said something else to her when I had the chance.

Like what?

I don't know. She picked up the sleeve again stared at the picture. Something more.

A week went past. I put the record on the moment I woke up and last thing before I went to bed and half a dozen times in between. Of the twelve tracks three were totally fucked even with nothing else between the record and the turntable mat. Another four needed a nudge. A couple of nudges one or two of them.

My affections shifted from day to day – from play to play sometimes – from Train From Kansas City to I Can Never Go Home Anymore to Give Us Your Blessings to Give Him (nudge) a Great Big Kiss to Remember (nudge nudge) (Walking in the Sand) to Out in the Streets.

He don't hang around with the gang no more

And he don't do the wild things that he did before ...

Between plays I was venturing out in the streets a bit more myself.

Hedda's apartment was on the third floor of a beige-bricked house – one of a pair: front doors shoulder-to-shoulder and flanked on their other sides by bay windows as far as the apartments above.

The street ran at a slight tilt. At the lower end was a small park that fell away quickly to the Hudson river. At the upper end was the Cathedral of St John the Divine. And running in between was Broadway.

I wasn't thick. I knew that was only a tiny bit of it. All the same: Broadway. Two hundred feet from my front door. There were traffic islands up the middle with plants growing in them and here and there wooden benches. I would gladly have sat there all day breathing in the smell of the air watching the taxis racing towards me on this side away from me on that ... except it was too hot to sit anywhere out of the shade for more than half an hour at a stretch.

I would give it a minute longer than I could strictly stick it.

Then I went back to the apartment switched the air conditioning on full blast and played the Shangri-Las.

Each time I came up the stairs the door in the apartment below ours opened just far enough for me to see beneath the chain an old man's face. You're not her he said. He sounded like a retired Bond villain. I'm her nephew I said. He shook his head and shut the door.

Hedda came home again one evening. Right in the middle of Leader of the Pack. Hair plastered to her forehead again. She stood with her back to the door shoulders heaving. I could tell as soon as I looked at her.

She was back in?

Hedda nodded.

And did you say something else to her – something more?

Hedda nodded.

Well?

It's her all right. *Margie* Ganser she said you call her not Marge. She admired my scarf. (Hedda's hand moved absently to touch it.) And the other two over the road the last time – that was them too – the Weisses: Betty and Mary only she didn't say Betty she said Liz.

She crossed the room to pick up the sleeve from the arm of the sofa next to where I had been lying.

I think that's the one wears the glasses now – in the middle. No wait – bringing the sleeve even closer – maybe on the right.

I threw myself back on the sofa and kicked my legs in the air. Only in New York!

There's a rehearsal room or something further down on 74th Street. They're all in there. The blond guy too.

I stopped kicking. Turned my head sideways. Rehearsing what?

She shrugged. Now *that* she said I didn't ask.

I went and took the record off the record player. It was hot. I checked the label again though I already knew what it said: *(P) 1966*. Eleven years ago.

I wonder how many more hits there've been since then.

None that I've ever heard.

Where do you think they've been all this time?

I don't know. Touring the world maybe.

What – by horse and cart?

Or maybe they just stopped for a while.

Maybe.

Next day when I got up I decided I was going to West 74th Street myself – on the off chance.

Hedda told me she had never ridden the subway the whole time she had been in New York and wasn't about to recommend I did either. I like things on the level she said. Only way I'm going underground is in a box.

Thirty-seven from where we lived – calculated by foot – turned out to be a punishing total. It was Broadway all the way dipping then rising then dipping again – the street and the state of the neighbourhoods bordering it – levelling out finally somewhere in the mid-eighties. Hedda's deli – I've got to say I was relieved to see it – was vast: a cross between a restaurant and a grocery store with a florist's out on the footpath for good measure. You never saw such an outrageous show of colour. It looked like Wonka Land had burst up through the paving. Hedda was putting cans on shelves way down at the back when I came through the door. She greeted me as though I had walked all the way from Belfast. You made it! She turned me by the shoulder and brought me back up so she could introduce me to everyone – the clerks and the countermen the bakers wiping hands on aprons before shaking ... the grill cook the short-order chef who was in fact short – introduced me too to the double row of hotplates up the centre of the floor towards the front from which nine-tenths of what I had eaten since I had been in New York had come. Hotplates Gem – Gem hotplates.

And then there was Rena.

Rena decided that Hedda was not taking care of me at all. Lookachoo. There ain't hardly nothing of you. She offered me my pick of the deli's fare then and there and seemed inclined to take it personally when I told her all I wanted was a drink.

She pursed her lips. Go head grab yourself a Gatorade then – knock yourself out.

I told her I had never heard of Gatorade and at once all was forgiven.

He ain't never heard of Gatorade? She looked accusingly at Hedda then laid a hand on my shoulder. Rena'll get you a lemon-lime.

It looked like something you would put in your car.

Tasted only slightly better.

I'm think I might save the rest for later I said.

You do that said Rena. And you come back any time whether that aunt of yours is here or not hear?

Outside again I turned about several times trying to get my bearings. I crossed over an avenue and walked twenty or thirty yards becoming more and more confused with every step. Spooked even. A year or two before I had sat – for the most part mute and as yet fully clothed – through all twenty-six episodes of *The World at War*. The nearest my mother and I ever came to regular Sunday observance. Looking at some of these buildings I realised with a creeping dread that I had witnessed families being marched at gunpoint out of their Central European twins – like that one there with green paint peeling from its high arched window frame or the one next to it with the enormous plant (rubber? cheese?) on a wooden stand – all of it even through the grime of the glass coated in dust abandoned by history.

Don't ask me how but I was certain then that whoever it was had come into the deli was winding Hedda up. Probably she got that all the time – do you know who you are the absolute spit of? – and was just getting a bit of her own back. Yeah sure I'm her. That's why I'm standing here searching in my purse for quarters for a slice of pizza.

I crossed over another avenue wider than the first putting a little of the strangeness behind me and carried on down across another avenue on the far side of which lay Central Park.

I wasn't thick but I could still make an honest mistake. I had thought the first couple of weeks I was there that

Central Park was the expanse of green I was looking down on from the railings at the back of the Cathedral of St John the Divine (or maybe that was the front though front or back there was a sheer drop down). And even then I had been pretty impressed. There was a lake in it and everything.

You could have fitted most of my own city's centre into where I found myself now – twice over – except of course then you'd have had to have gates put up around it; make everyone queue up to be searched before they got in. There was a road – a proper road: cars taxis buses – cutting through. The sound of trains came up from the gratings inside the low perimeter wall. The heat out here in the open was like all the summer days I had ever lived multiplied together with a damp blanket thrown on top to keep the air from moving. I thought of the oul lad who stood across the road from our City Hall in his gabardine and homburg hat in all seasons shouting into a megaphone hell is not a place of want hell is a place of plenty but the sinful not being able to feed themselves have not yet learned to feed each other. No they have not!

He might have been describing Central Park. Wherever I walked I could hear the sound of children crying could see dotted about the ground the ice creams that had melted before they reached the tongues that tried to lick them. Long strips of molten colour took on the solid form of roller-skaters drifting by before dissolving again a few yards on to lava-lamp apparitions. A dappled grey horse lay on its side a couple of feet from the upward-pointing shafts of an open-top carriage head and neck outstretched red plume wilted over one half-closed eye. A woman pushed a full-size pram with a fringed parasol where the hood should be and a large sleek-coated dog sitting up in it honking like a seal though I suppose there was an outside chance it was a seal that looked like a dog. Whatever it was it wanted down – down – down – down – but the moment its feet/flippers touched the ground it was clear it was too hot too fat too something to drag itself more than an inch or two so it honked to be lifted – up – up – up – then as soon as it was back in the pram started all over again honking to be let down and so you imagined it would go on – up and down up and down like something from a Greek myth – until the end of days. Even half an hour here was beyond me. My senses were fried before my skin was.

I cracked and drank the rest of the Gatorade.

I was walking back up to Hedda's deli – dragging myself like a mythic seal-dog – just beginning to wonder what I was doing here at all when I saw one of the sisters – Mary? Betty-make-that-Liz? – coming out of a place – just short of the first avenue I had crossed leaving the deli – that I had taken for shut up the previous time I had passed it: crumbling plasterwork shuttered windows reinforced door tiles missing from the door surround nearest the locks where someone had maybe tried just how reinforced the door actually was. All of which I can only think had combined with the temporary sense of being somewhere else entirely – some*when* – to distract me from the board between the door and the window frame with the name *Sire Records* and below that *Blue Horizon* next to the number 165.

Whichever sister it was stopped at the top of the steps to light a cigarette. (Even cigarettes were bigger here. The only people at home who had to reach that far in front of their faces to do anything were trombonists.) She had glasses – maybe the purple ones Hedda had talked about – pushed up into her hair then the door opened again and the other sister came out and plucked the glasses out of her hair as she passed – as though she had been the one who put them there in the first place which seeing as the one lighting the cigarette didn't object or even react might well have been the case. (She put them on and – yep: purple lenses.) Margie came last looking exactly as Hedda had described – exactly as she looked on the *Golden Hits* cover – right down to the white sleeveless top. It didn't seem possible that there could be eleven years between her then and now. Though seeing her – seeing them all – it was almost as hard to believe that they could have been responsible for the storm of heartache pain and flat-out joy that came out of the record player's speaker every time I lowered the needle.

A car pulled up at the kerbside next to a tree that looked about ready to give up the ghost. The car didn't look a whole lot better. The sisters and Margie came down the steps towards it. They all went to different doors as though each knew not only where she should go but where the others would go too – as though that was the thing they had been in that building rehearsing.

Thunk thunk thunk (even that had a rhythm) a spin of the wheels and they were away. Twenty seconds start to finish. I stood looking after the car – already at the junction waiting to turn right before a shop sign saying *Pioneer*. No one else on the street appeared even to have noticed. I could have believed I hadn't seen it myself. The fortress door opened and closed a fourth time. A blond-haired guy (*the* blond-haired guy?) stood at the top of the steps feeling in his jeans' pockets for something – money keys cigarettes – then satisfied whatever it was was there skipped down whistling like a man whose world could not get much better wheeling left when he hit the street coming straight for me. If he hadn't adjusted his feet in fact – a six-inch shuffle to the side – he would have walked smack into me planted as I was on the footpath like the woebegone tree.

I ran both my hands through my hair.

What just happened there?

The only thing I knew was I wanted to know more.

Hedda agreed to a temporary lifting of her number one embargo and the following morning I walked the further thirty blocks to Times Square. Every second sign said *Hot!* which was a statement of the obvious. Some of them said it two or three times and other things besides. *Real Sizzlers! Bizarre Action! Seeing is Believing! Everything 25C!*

I couldn't have been there more than five minutes – still trying to get my bearings – when a guy in shorts and a tie-dyed T-shirt approached me. Hey he said this is my spot.

Your spot for what?

Oh cute. Keep working that line. Just work it someplace else.

Hedda had told me the name of a second-hand store in a street running off the Square. If it's not the world's biggest selection of old books and tatty magazines she said it's the second. Anybody ever did have the time to read all the stuff in there they would probably find it added up to the sum total of humankind's achievements as well as sins.

You'll see a lot of stuff you probably shouldn't she told me but there are nuggets in among the dross …

An older man – white hair white moustache horn-rimmed glasses – came up to me in a canyon formed entirely of Westerns. He was holding a small magazine open at a centrefold that was all mouths and organs. (My impression was three times as many of the former as the latter.) What do you think about that he asked – huh?

I think you're lucky I don't call a cop. *I'm twelve years of age!*

It was a line Hedda had given me. Believe me she said they won't even think in that moment. They'll run a mile. The white-haired man didn't run. He did look genuinely stricken.

Hey kid I'm sorry. Hey an honest mistake. He folded the magazine shut. Offered me his hand. No hard feelings huh? We shook. I went back to my hunt. Which yielded at the end of another two-and-a-bit hours – out of that vast reservoir of human knowledge – a 1965 *Hit Parader* with a notice about a new Shangri-Las 45 Past Present and Future (Scratch Scratch and Scratchier on Hedda's LP). Some guy calling it the biggest record he had been associated with in his ninety-seven years in the record business. Which puzzled me. Not that I really believed he had been in the business that long or even that there had been a record business that long. I just couldn't understand why if the second part of the sentence was unreliable he expected anyone to believe the first. *You think you're not but you're selling it short. Selling the girls short.*

The girls.

Three of them again in the accompanying photograph. Except now there was only one Weiss sister – Mary – and it was Margie who was duplicated. And it was complete duplication. I couldn't tell the Gansers apart.

Hedda and I tried to figure it all out at home that night cross-referencing the text of the mag with the record sleeve. So two sets of two – Weisses and Gansers – one of each set – Mary Ann and Betty (who was also Liz) – apparently being from time to time surplus to requirements.

It's just like at the deli Hedda said. Tommy and Marv never work the same shift.

But you said you had seen them on TV the four of them together.

Yes and sometimes it's the day before Thanksgiving and it doesn't matter what your shift is normally: you all have to be there pitching in.

Where's Cambria Heights? I asked.

There was a street at home – Cambrai – that we pronounced Camberia. I thought Belfast had probably just messed up the spelling. We had a Sagimore Gardens that was supposed to be Sycamore next to Cyprus Avenue that should have been Cypress.

It's *Cam*-breea Hedda said. Why do you want to know?

It says in the magazine that's where they met. Andrew Jackson High School. Is it far do you think?

It's way way the other side of the river. Queens.

You couldn't walk it?

You couldn't walk it.

And she didn't need to add just entering the subway was going looking for trouble so that was an end to that.

Eat she said.

We were facing one another across the table a carton in the centre of it containing noodles another containing eggplant which I didn't know then had another name back home or even existed there any more than I knew that in its natural state it had a dark purple skin. Brown was how it looked in the deli carton – slimy – stuck all over with small black beans. I dug my fork in. I couldn't get enough of it.

I said to Hedda between mouthfuls I don't really look twelve do I?

She licked sauce off her forefinger and thumb and used them to tease a cigarette from its paper pack. About as much as I do she said.

To be honest I didn't know what she did look. Not twelve obviously but not as though she had seen her twenties come and (recently) go either. It was like she was standing right in the middle of the seesaw able to tilt it this way or that.

The next afternoon – Sunday – we managed to get a call through to my mother: two o'clock talking to seven one version of the 1970s talking to another with time lags and dropouts adding to the sense of mutual incomprehension … stop start stop start … you … no: you … what was that …? I was saying … I was saying … Sorry … I thought you'd finished … It doesn't matter … Finish … No.

This must be very expensive was what it was my mother was mainly trying to say.

It'd be expensive if all we talked about was how much it was costing Hedda said at last.

She had been holding the phone so we both had half an ear on it angling the mouthpiece as one after the other we spoke. Tried to speak. Here she said and made me take the receiver. The two of you have a minute on your own.

My mother began sobbing the instant Hedda was gone. Do you miss your mummy? Do you? Do you miss her?

I didn't know if I did. I do I said.

I'm glad. She sighed. Long long long. But you can't come home yet. You know that don't you?

Like I'd asked.

All right I said.

Big silence. I thought maybe she had dropped off the line altogether but no.

Is your Auntie Heather feeding you OK?

We had eggplant for dinner last night.

For the first time she laughed. In years it felt like. Are you having me on? Egg *plant*? What did you buy it with? Pennies from the money tr—

And then we really did lose the connection.

Hedda came and took the receiver from my hand and set it back on its cradle on the wall. I sometimes think it's worse than not talking at all she said.

I said nothing because what in all seriousness was there to say?

That night I set my travel alarm to get me up with Hedda.

I lay awake on the sofa in the morning until I heard her leave the bathroom. Or thought I did. When I pushed open the door she was standing ankle-deep in tissues before the mirror wearing only her bra and knickers though those registered only peripherally. A raised red line maybe half an inch wide ran from below her left shoulder blade to the last but one knobble of her spine before her knicker line. I didn't want to think what kind of a thing might have caused it.

She was looking at me out of the mirror.

What's the matter? You never see a woman without three pounds of make-up on her face before? Pass me that foundation at your feet and get the hell out of my way.

Next time I saw her the three pounds of make-up had been evenly and expertly distributed. She had on a camisole top that could have been custom-made to cover that raised red line: low at the back but not that low high at the waist but not quite that high.

Come on she said. I'll be late.

The door of the apartment below opened its customary six inches as we reached the first-floor landing. The old man who lived there fitted his face into the gap. Hedda gave him her full-beam smile – only me Mr Mogilevich – then even before the door was closed squinted her mouth my way. Poor guy must be up and down to that door fifty times a day.

I think he's been looking for you.

It's not me he's looking for. It's his daughter. Thinks every footstep on the stairs is her coming to see him.

From Russia?

Cincinnati.

She kept talking as we walked at speed down the last flight of stairs and into the street – into the heat that clung like head-to-toe shrink-wrap. I didn't catch the half of what she was saying. I couldn't shake the image of her at the bathroom mirror. I wasn't even started primary school when she came to live in America and had few memories of having seen her before she left. It was possible she had carried that mark all her life. But wouldn't there have been a story that went with it – a bit of family lore? *This one time your Auntie Heather was climbing a tree in Woodvale Park – couldn't have been more than five or six – and of course who was supposed to be looking after her but muggins here? And the next thing I heard this terrible crack …*

And then it occurred to me that the whole reason she was talking so much so fast was to stop me thinking or at least asking. So I came right out with it.

How did you get the scar?

For the first time since we left the apartment she drew breath – and started talking again immediately after as if she hadn't heard. I knew rightly but that she had. I knew rightly too that whatever had happened to her was no simple accident. The closest thing I could think was a whip: a *scourge*.

Was it him? Your ex?

We had reached a *DON'T WALK* sign. We didn't for a moment then – *WALK* – stepped out on to the road. She stopped unbidden on the other side and turned to me.

Things are never as straightforward as they look she said.

It's a fucking foot-long scar I wanted to say. How complicated can that possibly be?

But she was already walking again. I fell in beside her eventually and we completed the slog to West 74th Street in silence. I held the deli door for her. She hesitated a moment then kissed me on the cheek.

Scowling does your face no favours she said.

The oldest man I had ever seen in a baseball cap – and OK I hadn't before I came here seen that many young or old – was using a hose to spray the flowers out front and the footpath around them while talking to a man who was holding a sort of kazoo to his throat and belching.

Its – a – cop – Im – tell – ing – ya the kazoo man said: seven separate belches.

Even with the alien delivery I knew what he was talking about. The guy going around shooting people

– young couples – as they sat in their cars or on their porches. Son of Sam. Everybody had their theory.

I guess it could be said the old man in the cap.

Course – it – is – cops– cant – ne – ver – catch – cops.

The old man in the cap twitched his wrist and the spray from the hose turned mid-air and came down on the flowers at the far end of the display and the footpath beneath it. The smell of the damp dust whisked me briefly somewhere entirely other (but where? *where?* and how did New York keep doing that? were all big cities just a hodgepodge of smaller ones – smaller than small cities even more like thousands and thousands of other people's streets past as well as present all bundled up together?) so that when I returned to the present moment I was already level with the excuse for a tree just a few feet from the door of Number 165. I almost wished that I had come back a fraction of a second later – that the damp dust smell had carried me on up the front steps too far to turn back. As it was – standing there on the footpath – my courage or my gumption failed me. What would I say? And why hadn't I worked it out before I got anywhere near here?

I'd work it out now.

Better yet … I'd just wait.

I did.

Five minutes.

Ten.

Fuck.

Nobody in this city stood still that long. The cops' pale blue cars kept up a constant circuit – a little *whup* of

encouragement now and then from their sirens: keep it
moving there keep it moving.

I walked up and down a bit in part to look less
conspicuous and in part to give my legs something to do. I
checked the opening hours of the tailor further down the
street. I read the menu on the board outside the pizzeria
on the far side of the avenue that had *Pioneer* on the
corner (Columbus I knew now you called it) like it was
only a question of whether I went for square pie round pie
or white pie. (Actually what I wanted to know was why
they didn't have the only kind of pizza I'd ever heard of till
then: French-bread.) I kept circling back. That tree those
steps. That firmly shut door.

After a while I realised there was a girl my age-ish on
the other side of the street who had gone up and down
nearly as often as I had. She had what looked like a letter
in her hand that she appeared to be trying to deliver:
was it this building? No ... Maybe this? And here I was
to myself: I bet you anything in the world that letter is
nothing more than an empty envelope.

I tried a couple of times to catch her eye but she kept
turning her head away kept on walking up and down
up and down with an odd sort of stoop letting on to be
looking for a number that I was more convinced by the
second wasn't even written on the envelope or piece of
paper she was carrying.

As much to prove to myself I was right as anything
I crossed the street. She had a little army surplus bag
hanging from one shoulder and seeing me coming she

snatched it up in front of her. I thought for a moment she was showing me what she had painted (pretty hopelessly) on the flap: *Sidewinders*.

I have mace in here she said.

Good for you. I hadn't the first notion then what mace was. She lowered the bag – and her guard – a little. Even with the stoop and the way she had of angling her head so her fringe hung down shading her eyes she had two or three inches on me. You're not really trying to deliver a letter are you? I asked.

She scrunched up whatever was in her hand and shoved it under the flap of her bag. No and you're never going to go into that pizza joint either. (She actually said joint.)

So what are you really doing?

Same as you probably.

I looked at her a moment as she glanced across the road at the building I had seen the Shangri-Las come out of.

Would it be OK if I stood here with you?

Go ahead she said and almost at once loped off up the street and round the corner on to Amsterdam Avenue.

I thought that was probably the last I would see of her. There was a subway station about fifty yards away. She might not have a Hedda to advise her. She might have taken herself and the bag with the mace in it down there. But as suddenly as she had gone about half an hour later she came loping round the corner again. She stopped in front of me arms folded across her chest head tilted back. The fringe parted. So that's what grey eyes looked like.

I'm Vivien.

Gem.

She nodded as though it needed her approval.

From Scotland?

Close enough: Northern Ireland.

There's a *Northern* Ireland?

Oh you know only for the last fifty something years. Hedda had already told me there are essentially two types of Americans: the totally ignorant and the totally ignorant who think they aren't and want to send you home with guns.

Well there you are. She yawned and glanced down the street like she could care less about it – about what I thought of her for not knowing it – about what I thought about anything whatever – then she jerked her head back round to face me. How are you on North Carolina?

Well I couldn't draw you a map but I know it's there.

North Dakota?

Same.

North Virginia?

Yes.

She smiled. I wasn't going to give her the satisfaction of asking why.

A short time later she wandered off again – no nice talking or see you later: nothing – and this time didn't come back though she turned up again the next day *Sidewinders* bag bouncing off her hip about fifteen minutes after me. You missed nothing I was going to tell her but she started straight in before I got the chance.

Northern Ireland is where all the killing is right?

She had been doing some homework.

Right.

So is that why you're here? You're like some kind of refugee?

I felt my face go red. There's a bit more to it than that I said.

I had a vision of my mother in the hallway trying not to see me as she pleaded with her sister to take me off her hands.

Oh I get it Vivien said. Family shit. Folks?

Folk: there's just me and my mum.

It sounded more oh poor me than I meant it to.

At least you still got one she said.

Ah no listen I'm sorry.

She shrugged. Long long time ago now.

Her parents had died in a plane crash. Went away for a romantic weekend in Palm Springs and never came back. Vivien was only five at the time – staying with her grandparents while her parents were out of town. She could remember being brought into her grandmother's sitting room (it was that kind of a house – that size of a house: her grandparents had a sitting room each) the one with the sofa with gilt arms she was never allowed to sit on any time she visited and seeing her two younger brothers already sitting there – a space between them … Could remember her grandparents looking at the three of them trying to figure out what to do with them. She had been living with her grandparents ever since. You asked Vivien they still hadn't figured out what to do.

Which is to put in a few sentences what took her several dozen more and much scratching at the hinge of her chin and earlobe to tell me. Somewhere in the middle of it I realised I liked her. Liked her a lot.

Nothing much was happening that day either over the road if I had taken the time to notice. I had almost forgotten what we were standing around there for and then like that the blond-haired guy was there on the opposite footpath walking quickly hands in pockets.

Vivien gave a little yelp.

I looked from her to him.

Who is that?

Her head didn't move but her eyes slid round to me. Was I completely mad?

It's Andy.

Andy.

Paley.

He ran up the steps two at a time and knocked. Ten or more seconds passed in which Vivien didn't breathe at all.

So that's who she *is waiting for.*

Then the door was opened and he disappeared inside and she at last let go the breath she had been holding.

Andy Paley? she said again then held up the bag to me. The Sidewinders?

Would you believe me if I told you I never heard of either of them?

She came over all Rena-ish – hands to her cheeks mouth gaping. Forget all the killing; your life has been even more tragic than I thought she said. First LP I ever bought right? And there's a song on it – last track side one: Rendezvous – I mean I'm not totally deluded – she stood before me: she was totally something but not deluded – I didn't think he was saying to himself this is for Vivien when he was writing it. I mean it was five years ago for one thing so – well work that out – but I just had this feeling – no no feeling's not right this absolute certainty the moment I heard it right down in the pit of my stomach – he was talking to me … You know?

I knew.

She sang under her breath not to me or for me: for him for her and the connection between them. Rendez- rendez- rendez- rendez- rendezvous.

So I told her then about the Shangri-Las about Margie and the pizza slice and depends who you think I am about the *Golden Hits* Times Square the *thunk thunk thunk* of the car doors closing as off they went – for ever it was beginning to look like to me.

She was shaking her head. The Shangri-Las. *The Shangri-Las.* I thought they were all like about forty. I mean they are so black-and-white TV.

A cop car rolled round the corner one bare forearm visible at each side and all in between sunburst.

Let's go eat something Vivien said. You can tell me more.

I already told you all I know.

Let's eat anyway.

We ate seated on high stools at a counter before a window overlooking the little temple of a subway station at 72nd Street. Doughnuts: a box of six. Vivien had four to my two. She wouldn't let me pay for even one of them. Or for the chocolate milkshake.

You can buy me next time.

I liked that. Next time.

Deal.

Midway through the fourth she jabbed a doughnut segment towards the window.

Look out there she said.

I looked.

Notice anything?

I wouldn't have known where to start. Give me a clue here I said.

The people she prompted.

What about them?

Their height.

They're all different?

Not true. Not all. Look at those chicks – and those guys – and her in the hat – look at the guy she's with.

I followed where the less than half a doughnut (she had taken another bite) directed trying to work out what she was getting at then – whoa! – I saw it.

That is the weirdest thing.

It was as if everyone had paired off or bunched together with other people their own size. And once you saw it …

Wait: look at those – I started to say but had to break off to count them onetwothreefourfivesix – my god *seven*.

Young men in suits. Straight out of the five-foot-nine factory. You could have laid a pole across their heads and it wouldn't have slid off.

What'd I tell you! Vivien said. Opposites attract? My ass they do. Sames attract! People want to hang out with people exactly like themselves.

I asked her – only half putting it on – if that meant our own chances of friendship were doomed.

Phuh! was all she said – all she could say the last of the doughnut now being in her mouth. She took a slurp of milkshake to clear it. When I say *people* I mean lazy people: people who don't want to think too hard.

Back round on 74th Street at some point in the afternoon Andy came out and stood on the footpath directly facing us.

Vivien's yelp was closer to a whimper.

Why don't you go and say hello?

What do you think I am a freak?

All right *I* will.

She grabbed the back of my trousers twisting them in her fist. Do and I swear I will kill you right here.

Her face was immobile with fear. Come on I said he's waiting for *something*. I crooned the words she had sung earlier. Rendez- rendez- rendez- rendez- rendez- rendezvous.

She gave my trousers another twist which had the desired effect. At almost the same moment a cab pulled up. The door opened and a guy stepped out and – fuck a duck – it was uncanny … I glanced round – Vivien's face

… the fear was replaced by something more like awe.

Oh my sweet Jesus she said: there's … there's …

Two of them.

Only this one – the brother (for there was no way they were not brothers) – was younger – taller – blonder – handsomer: head to toe and in every respect just –*er*.

He put his hand on Andy's shoulder as they walked back up the steps together and stood talking in the doorway a moment before going inside.

I think I need to go and find a place to lie down Vivien said and she staggered off. I wondered from the way she was walking whether she hadn't actually peed herself a little.

Either way she missed the Shangri-Las arrive – less than ten minutes after she went – talking among themselves and across one another. They gave the impression they were making up for lost time or trying to cram everything in to the time they had – like they expected at any moment to lose the connection.

(Are you having me on? *Egg*-plant …)

I hung back a couple of minutes after they went in then walked across and stood right up against the rail separating the footpath from the basement steps straining to listen. I thought at one moment I could hear a piano – no I *could* hear a piano: getting louder … and louder … and passing behind me at full volume. Car radio. After it had gone there was just the sound of the street again.

Still they had come back. It seemed reasonable to expect they would be back again.

I walked to the end of the street and took a right for home.

Next day was one of those days when the serial killer took the headlines. A couple shot in their car in Brooklyn overnight. The early news was confused but it wasn't looking good for either of them. I knew the grammar of incidents like this inside out: first came the not looking good then came the man injured in last Tuesday's gun attack by this or that organisation in such and such a place ... has died. The longer the sentence went on the less chance there was the victim had pulled through. In this instance over in Brooklyn the man did survive but the woman he had met just four days before and was in the car with – windows wound down – because even at midnight it was hot like you wouldn't believe

died

Stacy Moskowitz her name was. She was twenty years of age.

Hedda said it would make anyone think twice before going on a date. I was – guiltily – sort of glad to hear it. I had begun to think the reason she never went anywhere was that I was there cramping her style. I could count on the fingers of one hand the nights she had been out since I came to live with her. Actually I could count on three-fifths of them. And two of those had been to the movies with Rena. This was a woman barely out of her twenties – not defeated-looking as her sister my mother already seemed to seven-years-younger-me to be at that age. (That admittedly would have been around the time we had to move house.) She could have been in magazines. Even before she left Belfast she had been asked – that most definitely was a part of family lore. The man who had come up to her at the bus stop one day ... *Highly unusual I know and your parents I know might be sceptical ...* Which was putting it mildly.

No daughter of mine is going to flaunt herself.

Daddy it's knitting patterns!

Aye it starts there. Who knows where it stops.

The one time I had mentioned to her though that I didn't want her staying in nights on my account she told me not to flatter myself.

People at home think because it's New York the opportunities are endless she said and maybe they are but not always the right ones.

I had the bathroom tidied in time for her getting home. I had the oven on too.

Chicken over rice. It sounded like nothing much but there were peas and carrots in the rice – *erbs* (the word had lost its h here) – onion cooked so long it was almost toffee on top of the chicken and over it and the rice both was the white sauce Hedda had carried home in its own little carton.

I've made a friend I said when we had finished eating. Vivien.

Vivien he or Vivien she?

She.

Hedda raised an eyebrow. A girlfriend?

A friend who is a girl.

That's nice for you she said. Whereabouts does she live?

With her grandparents.

Oh well then I'll know where to find you if I need you.

I get the feeling it's somewhere pretty posh. Her grandparents have their own sitting rooms.

That's one thing New York isn't short of – posh places to live. I'm sure she's very nice. Just don't go getting into any cars with her. Don't think I'm kidding you either.

My friend who was a girl brought back word next day – wherever she unearthed it – that Andy Paley's brother was called Jonathan.

Turns out he's a musician too she said. They're making a record together.

It seemed that was what you did that summer in New York if you had a sibling and could hold a tune.

I can't imagine wanting to sit in a small room every day with my brothers Vivien said or sisters for that matter.

I didn't know you had sisters.

What?

When you were telling me about your grandparents' apartment sitting on that sofa with the gilt arms – you said you and your brothers.

My sisters are a lot younger. They were probably already in bed.

I nodded. I guessed if she was five then … It was on the tip of my tongue to say I couldn't imagine having any sisters or brothers whether I was sitting all day in a room with them or not. Maybe that's why Mary Ann isn't there I did say.

Yeah I was going to tell you that too Vivien said. Mary Ann's dead.

No I said. No what it is you see sometimes there were four of them and sometimes three – Mary Liz and Margie – but other times it was Mary Margie and Mary Ann: it kept changing.

I'm telling you what I read that's all.

When?

Did I read it?

Did she …?

Oh right. Couple of years ago.

And suddenly the sister or brother I couldn't imagine a second or two before even having was there and gone. No matter how much you let on you couldn't stand them – maybe didn't have to let on maybe genuinely thought you really really couldn't – for them suddenly just not to be there … the ache.

I wiped my eyes and my stare – blank until then – became focused again on the front of Number 165.

That's it isn't it? I said. Sire Records.

Vivien clapped her hands slowly. Let me be the first to congratulate you on your reading ability.

I mean that's the whole of it.

Far as I know.

It's funny. Everything's so much bigger over here but then every now and then it's all flipped on its head. I thought record companies were like the BBC. You know?

What's the BBC like?

In Belfast? If she had asked me a couple of years before I could have told her there were sandbags out the front.

Grander I said. Doormen. A bit of – I don't know how to say it: pomp.

Pomp she said back in my own accent. A stone dropped into deep water. You'd maybe get more of that at CBS.

All that is is steps and a door.

Pretty much.

No intercom even.

Huh she said. No intercom.

I can't believe I never heard that Hedda said for maybe the fifth or sixth time. You're sure that friend of yours knows what she's talking about?

She sounded pretty certain.

No wonder they've been away all this time.

We had walked up on to Broadway together when she got home from the deli to pick up some things for the house. Washing powder scouring pads other sorts of pads – avert your eyes Hedda said too late – a sack almost of cotton wool.

The word did not seem to have filtered through here that it was past six o'clock. Way past. The street teemed with the kind of after-work life that was or had become alien at home.

In Belfast by this stage you'd be lucky to find a filling station with its doors open or anything more than a packet of peanuts and an air freshener for sale.

We called at a laundromat to pick up a bedspread that was too big for the machine in the apartment.

An elderly woman was leaving as we were coming in. Not an inch above four foot six if you took away the hat – an inverted basket with its produce stuck around the outside: red berries black grapes varieties of greenery.

Mrs Mogilevich Hedda said. How's Mr Mogilevich?

Old said Mrs Mogilevich. We're both old.

Nonsense you'll outlast the lot of us. Gem: the door.

I held it open. For all the notice Mrs Mogilevich took.

Hedda shook her head. She's not looking good at all that wee woman.

I had just let go the door handle when … What's *that*? I said.

Strange squelching sounds were coming from somewhere in the back of the shop. It was a moment or two before I could separate them entirely from the sound of the machines or untangle the odd wailing I had also detected from the high-pitched whine of the driers but soon they had combined to fill the whole room. They were to spread out from that moment – that laundromat – until eventually they seemed to seep into every corner of the city and the summer I feel luh uh uh uhv I feel luh uh uh uhv I feeeel *love*. Nothing else came as close to deflecting me from the Shangri-La path I trod.

Vivien and I soon worked out a rough timetable for the rehearsals – the recordings as we now assumed them to be. Andy was first to arrive most days just before eleven usually on foot – always that can-you-actually-believe-this? expression on his face – bounding up the steps fifteen twenty minutes ahead of Margie Mary and Liz who arrived in the car that maybe – the more cars I saw to compare it with – wasn't especially bashed-up looking. (The roads in places resembled more the raw materials from which roads would eventually be made. They would have done for *any* car never mind one whose front end and back end were barely in the same time zone and could hit two potholes simultaneously.) They came out again most days in reverse order – them before him – sometime after five when Vivien and I would just happen to be passing on the other side of the street.

We got so we could judge the mood in a glance. That looks like it went all right one of us would say to the other under our breath or now and then – the force and angle say of a jet of cigarette smoke the snap of a lighter lid – oh dear better luck tomorrow.

Between however many past eleven and something after five we had time on our hands.

It seemed to make sense we would spend it together. Try and work out exactly what it was we wanted from all of this hanging around.

Not a lousy autograph that's for sure Vivien said.

Christ no. Not an autograph.

But what?

That was the big question.

What.

Whatever we did in those hours in between Vivien – despite her *next time* once upon a time – insisted on paying. Hey she said you're helping me out here. The only way her grandparents knew how to communicate with her was by giving her money. They would have taken it as a slap in the face if she had brought a single cent of her allowance home.

We ate a lot of doughnuts. They seemed to form the larger part of Vivien's diet. Only the number differed depending on the time of day. The four she had eaten that first time she treated me signified something like lunch.

And then there were the things she just bought me out of the blue. Orientation gifts she called them. One day she turned up with a copy of the Gettysburg Address in a leather slipcase the next with a bag full of sweets and chocolate bars for me to try. We need to do this properly she said and handed me a card she had managed to get printed up with the names of the sweets in a column and the numbers one to ten running along the top. (Abba-Zaba was a distant last. On the list of things I have eaten in my entire life Abba-Zaba could well be in the bottom three.)

She introduced me too to thrift stores which were either legion in that end of town or plotted somewhere on a map that Vivien had learned by heart. New clothes were a con – *obviously* – but there was more to thrift-store shopping than that. This was not a question of discovery but reunion.

You got a feel she said as soon as you walked in the door.

No – not here – not today ... Not here ... Not here either.

But then – store number four say – Hmm yes I'm sure I left something in here she would say as she walked along the racks fingertips dancing ahead of her. I'm sure I'm sure I'm sure ... Ah look – stopping – unhooking the hanger from the rail – there it is!

It could be anything at all: a dress a shirt a sweater jeans. Didn't matter how unlikely or dowdy. She would put it on and she was right it looked like it had been hanging there all this time waiting on her coming back to pick it up. One day it was a pair of white wet-look hot pants that I'd pulled out of a pile for a laugh thinking she would run a mile from them.

Oh yeah *those* she said and took them from my hand and straight in behind the tatty curtain that stood in for a changing room.

She walked out again a minute later and stood right in front of me hands on hips. See?

I saw.

I saw she saw I saw.

She turned up next day wearing them and carrying a new copy of the *Golden Hits of The Shangri-Las*. If I'm going to have to listen to them I want to listen to them right: no scratches or skipping.

It took me a moment to catch on. I'm guessing we can't play it round at your grandparents'? She shook her head. No-o-o. Right then I said.

We didn't say anything more about it either of us but on the long walk up to the apartment (your aunt is a freaking nut – you know that right?) I think we both accepted what was going to happen once we got there.

Mr Mogilevich came to the door of his apartment as we hit the first-floor landing. You're not her he said to Vivien. She shook her head. Sorry to disappoint you. He watched us all the way up the stairs – more wistful I thought looking back and seeing his expression than reproachful. I think he had maybe arrived at the same conclusion Vivien and I had.

We sat legs crossed facing one another on the sofa. The sheet I slept on was still tucked in around the cushions. I forgot some days to take it off.

Have you done this before? she asked.

Yes. You?

Yes.

That's a relief.

For both of us.

And then without further preamble she leaned forward and kissed me and – well – one thing followed another and another and then a whole lot of other things followed in rapid succession and then I lost all track of what and who and where exactly and how long.

Afterwards I asked her if she had been telling the truth about doing it before.

No.

I sort of thought.

We had slipped down on to the floor taking sheet and cushions with us.

Were you? she said.

My head was resting on her collarbone.

No.

I sort of thought that too. Well it was nice to get it out of the way.

I know what you mean.

And it wasn't terrible.

Maybe for you it wasn't.

She cuffed me round the back of the head. Then kissed where she had cuffed.

Protective.

I wasn't sure whether you were gay.

Me and all. (The picture in the mag that time – part of me had wanted to say show me more *show me more*.)

What do you think now?

It's early days.

She wound the sheet tight around her. Play me some music.

I crawled across the floor to where the record lay. She laughed. I looked back down the length of my bony-arsed self.

What?

You really don't care do you? I thought people in Ireland were all screwed up with guilt and shame.

Don't worry I'm screwed up too. Just not with that.

I tipped up the inner sleeve (there was an inner sleeve!) and let the rim of the record come to rest against the heel of my hand reaching up with my middle finger for the label. I don't think I had ever until that moment held a brand-new record.

I had to stop myself leaning forward and licking it.

Are you ready? I asked her.

Just put the fucking needle down!

We listened to Leader of the Pack. We listened to Past Present and Future. Even on that record player of Hedda's with its needle as blunt as an elbow in a tweed jacket they sounded like treasures restored. The Train From Kansas City came and went – Heaven Only Knows – Remember (Walking in the Sand) whose *softly softly we kiss* made me think of a house you had known all your life that you suddenly discovered had a secret staircase going down down down below the ground …

I turned to Vivien when it was over. I can't tell you how many times I have listened to that song I said ...

She shushed me. I'm still listening.

I stopped then listened with her while side one played out. As soon as it was finished she scuttled across on all fours forgetting any shame of her own and plonked the needle down again at the fading waves of Remember then it was woo-oo-oo-woo ...

He don't hang around with the gang no more ...

Vivien returned to my side. Laid her head back against the frame of the sofa.

That's the song.

Mary's voice found another level: *cause I know that he did it for me ... his heart is out in the street.*

That's the song I'll think of if I think of you.

Which took the wind out of my sails a bit. *If?*

I slid in closer to her rested my head on her shoulder watching the skin at the base of her neck tremble as she drew in breath then slowly slowly let it out again.

I'm going to stay here and get a job I told her.

The skin moved more rapidly. Yeah well I'm going to travel the world soon as I have the money.

The way you spend it?

Proper money. It's been in a trust since my folks died. The minute that comes through ... So long America!

Come to Belfast.

He grew up on the sidewalk streetlight shining above. He grew up with no one to love ...

What's the point if you're going to be here?

I'd go back for that. I'd take you all over the place. Though as I said it I realised that I had no idea what all over even entailed – that I knew as much really of my own city as I knew of New York. Which was to say next to nothing at all.

I'll let you know if I change my mind she said but from her tone I thought no you won't. And now – she started putting on her clothes – if you will excuse me I have an appointment with a minor rock star.

I told her I was coming with her. No you're not she said. It's part of the ritual. I have to walk by myself and feel the world transformed: the end of innocence.

And what about me?

You could always carve a notch in your bedpost.

You're leaning against it.

Or – she pushed me off her as she stood – you could wash that sheet.

I lifted the record between the middle of both palms and carefully turned it over while she just as carefully finished dressing. She walked out the door to Sophisticated Boom Boom. You'd nearly think she had waited for the cue.

You missed a trick today Hedda was already saying as she came through the door. She stopped. Looked at me struggling to fold a just-washed sheet. You're doing the laundry now too?

Just trying to help … What trick?

Here – she let the bag slide off her shoulder and took one end of the sheet. Singing on the street she said as she walked her end towards me.

Our faces were two inches apart.

No!

Apparently. I missed it too. Woman in buying a meatball sandwich told us. Didn't know who they were just three girls and a guy pretending to conduct but beautiful like you wouldn't believe she said – she actually stopped a minute to listen – she thought maybe they were having their photos taken: there was another woman hanging round with a camera … and here's you at home doing the housework.

She bent to pick up her bag. There's just going to be no living without you is there?

You don't need to worry I said because I've decided to stay.

She stopped halfway to the kitchen. It's not quite as easy as that.

You did it.

I got married.

I'll find a way.

Oh Gem.

What?

A moment – a sigh – let's get some dinner she said.

She unpacked the cartons. I got the knives and forks.

Shortly after that the cops up in Yonkers (it was more adverb than place name: downtown – midtown – uptown – yonkers) arrested the guy who had been shooting all the young people sitting in porches and parked cars. He was only a couple of years older than most of his victims. And his father wasn't called Sam. His neighbour's dog was though.

His story was it was this dog that had instructed him to carry out the shootings. What can I say? Coming from where I had come from it didn't sound all that farfetched. Why not a dog in fact? At least you could see and hear it. Don't ask me how history spoke or gave instructions for someone to cut a guy's throat and dump him in an alleyway or leave a bomb under a table in a packed café on a Saturday afternoon.

I had come into the Son of Sam story too late ever to get completely caught up in the panic but even I could feel a weight lifted. Now there were just the everyday murders and mayhem to contend with – oh and the fact that the whole city looked about ready to fall apart at any moment and that the dial on the heat setting seemed permanently jammed at infernal.

I asked Hedda that night: Do you think maybe now you'll start dating again?

Oh sure. Where did I put that waiting list of men?

I bet if they knew you were available they'd be queued round the block.

Available! You make it sound like a room to let. What do you want me to do take out an ad?

You could stop wearing your wedding ring I nearly said. She still wore it most days. Why shouldn't I? she had said the one time I had mentioned it before. It's a beautiful piece of jewellery. She wasn't wrong about that.

You have to know your own worth she said. Otherwise how do you expect anybody else to? I'm happy as I am for now.

She had her legs tucked up underneath her. The night's wine was more half-begun than done. If she stopped now she'd probably stay happy too – at least until tomorrow night. She finished what was in her glass. Poured another: larger.

A Girl Called Dusty came out.

Colour Hedda gone.

I woke up that night to a terrible howling. Hedda passed the foot of the sofa pulling an old sweater on over her nightdress. The howling got worse when she opened the door echoing off the walls of the stairwell. She walked out into it leaving the door ajar. By the time she returned less than a minute later I had already got up and got on me.

It's Mr Mogilevich she said.

Mister?

Heart attack looks like. The ambulance is on its way. Go you down to the street and make sure they get the right door. She came out of her room again in her dressing gown tucking a fresh pack of cigarettes into the pocket getting ready for the long haul.

The ambulance was already out front when I got down. The hospital was less than half a mile away. A couple of paramedics in green tunics pushed past me in the vestibule with their cardiac-arrest gear. I ran up the stairs behind them. They practically fell into the Mogileviches' apartment. I held back. All I could see was the back of their tunics and Mr Mogilevich's feet and ankles. I knew just by the colour of them it was already too late.

Mrs Mogilevich had heard a noise and got of bed: I couldn't remember where I'd left my slippers she said or maybe I'd have got to him sooner.

She found him in the hallway – lying exactly as he was when the paramedics were trying and trying and eventually failing to revive him. Whatever he had heard or thought he had heard himself at half two in the morning he must have been on his way to open the door.

I don't know how many times I told him Mrs Mogilevich said: *It's not her.*

Hedda sat with her the rest of the night and into the morning – phoned herself in sick to the deli – and only left when the daughter arrived at last at three in the afternoon from Cincinnati.

Piece of work was Hedda's verdict. You would think to hear her he had gone and died just to mess up her diary. Maybe if you had come and visited him sooner – she said it as though it was the daughter standing before her not me – maybe if you had picked up a phone once in a while …

She stopped herself. Ah nuts. Not my family not my business.

I wasn't exactly in a hurry to go back down there myself. When Hedda told me that evening she was going to join other neighbours paying their respects I said I would stay where I was; make sure everything was all right in our apartment.

I'm only downstairs. What do you think's going to happen? No – you're coming with me.

I hardly even knew the man.

You've been living above him the past month and a half.

Yeah but …

What?

I just feel a bit wick. I've never done anything like this.

Never? Well then consider it part of your education. Besides it might interest you to know that the people down there will have other things on their mind than whether or not you're uncomfortable.

The door was opened to us by the Korean man who shared a landing with the Mogileviches. Other neighbours were already inside as Hedda said offering support. And cheesecake. You never in your life saw so many cheesecakes: thick as car tyres and half as wide again. And the smoke! There were distinct strata of it – pale grey close to the floor brown at head height blue towards the ceiling. Nowhere was it denser than in the corner where the daughter sat (I knew her without having to be told) side on to a table – shoulder angled to repel – giving every impression she wished she was still in Cincinnati. She must have worked her way through half a pack in the less than forty minutes we were there. If she spoke five words that was the height of it.

Mrs Mogilevich sat in an armchair flanked by two straight-backed wooden chairs in which neighbours took turns to sit. She swapped a Kleenex from one fist to the other pressing it now to this eye now to that until there was next to nothing of the Kleenex to swap though she carried on with the hand motions dabbing with decreasing effect. Fifty-three years she kept saying. Fifty-three years … What am I supposed to do now?

Another woman I'd never seen before – from the floor above us Hedda told me afterwards – moved into one of the wooden chairs. She declared to the room as much as Mrs Mogilevich that she had only had her husband three years before the War began and had lived without him now more than ten times that long.

You tell yourself you won't forget a single thing about him she said but with every year – every day – another little bit goes. Sometimes I ask myself did I just dream him up. You know?

More neighbours arrived more cheesecake. The woman who wondered if she had dreamt up her husband was smuggled out of the way. Then it was Hedda's turn and mine in the chairs. I took the old woman's hand and shook it awkwardly – it was still closed in a fist and damp. Sorry was the only word I was able to get out. Hedda though leaned in taking her in her arms and spoke low close to her ear. The hand I had briefly held suddenly gripped the leg of my trousers just above the knee getting hold of a bit of skin in the process. I couldn't tell whether Mrs Mogilevich even knew she was doing it but there was nothing I could do in response but grit my teeth and wait. When she and Hedda broke apart their faces were stained with one another's tears. Mrs Mogilevich smiled – nodded – let go of my trouser (my leg) finally.

Am I allowed to ask you what you said to her? I – all right: *asked* when Hedda and I were on our own landing again.

I always say the same thing – the thing an old man said to me when your granny died: Keep the faith.

That's all?

I was thinking of that hand gripping my leg. How long it went on.

You have to keep whispering it.

I don't think I'd ever really thought of you as religious.

Religion's got nothing to do with it she said. Just hang in there that's all it means. That's all any of us can do – she let us into the apartment threw herself on the sofa – and God knows Mrs Mogilevich is going to need to with that bitch of a daughter.

Mr Mogilevich wasn't cold when Elvis keeled over on his toilet down in Memphis Tennessee and died. Heart attack again: brought on in Elvis's case by prescription drugs or constipation was the word. I was going for constipation. The photos the papers ran of him in his final days looked like he had eaten the younger version of himself. From his expression it didn't agree with him.

Hedda could only find one record – a 45 – on her rack. Burning Love. She wiped the dust off with the sleeve of her blouse: a rare courtesy. We listened in respectful silence for two minutes forty seconds. The tone arm rose and returned – stuttering – to its cradle. Hedda's nose wrinkled. It's probably sacrilege to say it today of all days but I never really got him. He was always a bit – a movement of her shoulders. Not quite a shrug more an effort – fruitless finally – to frame the words – *you know.*

I sort of thought I did better than if she had been able to come right out and say it.

We gave the B-side a go. The intro sounded like something you'd hear leaking out of a meeting hall back home. It's a matter of time before I go back there Elvis sang. He was righter than he knew. Twenty seconds and the record was off the turntable and in its sleeve.

Mind if I put on the Shangri-Las?

Be my guest!

Vivien said her first thought had been for Elvis's daughter – losing her daddy like that.

I could have kicked myself for not thinking that was how she was bound to see it. I could have kicked myself even harder for having said the thing about him looking at the end as though he had eaten the younger version of himself.

I mean she said she's what: eight?

Nine. I suppose at least she had him for those few extra years.

No! Vivien said it so loud I actually jumped. That's much much worse. She got to know him. What do you remember from when you were that age? Lots I bet. I can hardly remember anything about my folks and I tell you what else I prefer it that way.

I was still trying to think how to recover from my faux pas squared when she dug me in the ribs.

M-A-R-Y she said. Don't look … No: do.

I did.

Mary had come out to lean against the rail next to the door of Number 165. It was the first time in all the hours we had been there that one of the group appeared without the other two following right behind. She wasn't on her own though. She was talking to a guy who we had seen a couple of times before with Andy: curtains of shoulder-length brown hair big soulful eyes made bigger by his granny specs. Or mostly he was talking and she was listening – head a little bowed – nodding

That guy really really digs her said Vivien. But she doesn't dig him. Not the same way … at least not any more.

You can tell all that from here?

The surprise to me is that you can't. Watch.

He had dipped his head now level with hers. Mary touched his hand lightly stopping him. She's saying whatever there was between us is over Vivien interpreted. She's saying I'd better get back inside.

He hesitated as though uncertain whether he should follow but Mary was already halfway to the door. He looked about him as much as to check whether anybody had seen. He looked at Vivien and me standing across the way. He pushed his glasses back against the bridge of his nose. Then he beat it on down the steps and out of there.

I think you could well be right Detective I said.

I asked her if she wanted to come back with me to Hedda's apartment.

You have a look on your face like you're going to propose to me.

I felt myself blush.

Oh come on I was joking she said and a minute later with a nudge of the shoulder: some other time – I'd like to do that again.

Yeah well I'll have to see if I can fit you in my diary.

She went to give me a hug that ended up a headlock.

I was walking home by Central Park West when a voice rang out from the other side of the street.

Hey! Kid!

It was him: granny specs.

I glanced around to see which of the actual kids on the street and on the park side of the wall he was calling to then realised – yeah you – he meant me.

He stood his ground. Clearly if we were to talk I was going to have to go to him. I thought about not bothering my head. He would want to know what all I had seen or heard or heard Vivien say she knew he said earlier. He made a sweeping motion with his arm: get over here.

What the hell. It wasn't like I had anywhere else I needed to be.

At the next break in the traffic I jogged across.

He put his hands in his jeans pockets. Or at least (even for the times those were some pretty tight jeans he had on him) his fingers.

What's your name?

Gem.

He nodded. He didn't tell me his.

You're always there aren't you: you and your girlfriend?

She's not my girlfriend. Not like …

I couldn't think of the right comparison. He shrugged. It was all one to him.

So what have you got?

I don't know what you mean. I thought maybe he had misinterpreted the line about Vivien not being my girlfriend.

I figured hanging around outside a record company he said you had to have a demo or a song at least.

Yeah right.

What age are you? Fourteen? Fifteen?

It was an improvement on twelve.

Sixteen – then in case he thought I was very small for my age – just.

Sixteen. He nodded weighing it up. I'd written Walk Away Renee by the time I was your age.

Even I knew Walk Away Renee. My mother sang it. I wouldn't have been surprised if her mother had sung it. There was no way on earth this guy had anything to do with it never mind that he hadn't sounded like he was boasting when he said it. Perplexed more like.

I was going to say if you wanted me to – you know – take a tape into the people there. But since you don't have anything.

He pulled one hand from his pocket. So long it said. He started walking.

Here did you really write that? I called.

He stopped. Turned again. And more he said.

Like he couldn't imagine how himself.

I let myself into the apartment to find a man sitting there
tie loosened suit jacket slung over the back of the sofa
right ankle resting on his left knee. Or it had been resting.
It jiggled when he saw me. By his good looks did I know
him: Hedda hadn't been exaggerating.

You're the nephew he said.

That's right.

He took a draw on his cigarette. Blew the smoke out
the corner of his mouth.

I'm the ex-husband.

I guessed. Does Hedda know you're here?

He snorted. Hedda! You know where she got that
right? You know her Irish friends all used to call her
Header? That's a crazy person where you're from right?
Nuts. She didn't like it when I started calling her it in
front of other people.

He gave the cigarette a limp-wristed wave mimicking
her trying to cover over the slur. It's *Hedda* ...

I walked round behind him into the kitchen got a
Coke from the icebox and flipped the lid on the opener
next to the sink. I held the bottle to my cheek closing my
eyes. Just go I was saying to him inside my head.

Don't mind me he called back over his shoulder. I just
pay for all this.

I went and sat facing him swigging from the Coke
every now and then. Neither of us spoke.

Hedda came in a short time later. She stopped in
the doorway.

When did you get in? she asked him. Not how: when.

A couple of hours ago. I'd been thinking about taking a nap but your nephew here had me spellbound with his dazzling conversation.

Wait is he staying here? I asked Hedda.

No *he* isn't he said. Not that it's any goddamned business of yours either way.

Hedda stood looking from one of us to the other her chest rising and falling. She turned and went into the bathroom.

Give me a couple of minutes to get washed and changed she said and shut the door.

He called after her. You know where I am if you need a hand!

His smirk as he looked at me … I stayed in the room with it as long as I could bear.

Hey don't take it so hard he said as I left.

The temperature out had dropped maybe half of one degree though there was a slight breeze too coming up from the river and – take my word – compared to the atmosphere inside half a degree and slight breeze was like a welcoming plunge into a cold bath. I took a couple of turns around the block.

When I came back an hour later they were both gone. I sat in the seat where your man had sat crossing my right ankle over my left knee. Smirked. I'm the ex-husband I said aloud and slapped the cushion.

Fucker.

I heard Hedda come in some time after one. Three goes it took her to get the key in the lock. She kicked off her shoes in the doorway – a hand resting on the wall for much-needed support. I let her get as far as her own bedroom door.

I don't believe you I said then.

She stopped. I waited for her to say something – anything at all – but she didn't. Just went in and closed the door behind her. Then fell on to her bed.

Ooof

All the way down the street I was changing my mind about what to tell Vivien first. The guy with the granny specs who was talking to Mary … My aunt's ex-husband – the wife beater … He thought we were in a band … One o'clock in the morning … I should have just told him we were … kept my mouth shut.

I turned left into West 74th.

Shit.

A pair of cop cars were parked in V formation against the kerb on the far side. Vivien was getting into the car nearest to me – a cop's hand spread open pressing down on the top of her head. He had to reach up.

I went to run out but a delivery van pulled up right in front of me then a guy jumped down getting in my way as I tried to go round the back.

Hey what's the idea? he said.

I turned around – went the other way. The cop car door was already closed and the cop was back in the passenger seat slapping the dashboard: *that's us.*

I shouted: *Vivien!*

If she heard me she didn't even turn her head. The car pulled away with a little *whup* of the siren. Like it just slipped out. Like there ought to have been a smell went with it.

Another cop leaned on the open door of the second car – one foot on the road one foot on the door trim – looking after the first car smiling admiringly. New York's streets just got that little bit safer.

Where are they taking her? I asked.

That depends on whether her parents decide they'll have her back – The siren *whupped* again as the car with de-orphaned Vivien in it nosed out on to Amsterdam Avenue – Ran away from home with two thousand of their hard-earned dollars.

That's hilarious I said. Of all the millions of things I might have said. I didn't find it funny in the slightest. *Parents!* I actually felt like giving her a slap.

The cop's eyes slid round on to me. Hilarious? he said. You think? She a friend of yours?

He took his arm off the car door hitched his belt: on the case again. And where do you live? he asked.

You probably wouldn't know it.

Oh no?

Finaghy.

I was right. He didn't.

It's near Dunmurry.

He got then what I was up to. Where in New York wise guy?

In my aunt's apartment.

That did it. All right he said. Name?

Hedda.

His forehead collapsed like a wet cardboard box.

I thought you meant *her* name I would have said if his car radio hadn't suddenly started up fizzing and bleeping and spitting out bits of words. Harsh. Broken. The cop leaned into the car to answer. I took advantage of his back being turned to start walking. I didn't know whether the Gettysburg Address the *Golden Hits of The Shangri-Las* and all those doughnuts and candy bars made me an accessory. I got as far as the corner before I risked a look back and then only long enough to determine that he was still on his radio. One of the few truths that held as absolutely on this side of the Atlantic as the other – to the north of it and even to the south: no good ever came from volunteering more information than you absolutely had to to the police.

I had gone another twenty or thirty yards when the realisation hit me. I ran back. The cop car was pulling away. Whatever those bits of words from the radio added up to had elbowed me from the forefront of the cop's mind.

Hold on I said. She *is* a friend … Take me with you!

I chased it as far as the corner then stood on the kerb and shouted through cupped hands. Where do her parents live? *Where do they live?*

Down the street another car had drawn up to the kerb. *Thunk thunk thunk.* Don't ask me how but I knew without looking the three of them were staring at me. Don't ask me why but at that moment I didn't care to turn around.

I lost all track of time as I walked. I lost all track of place. I found myself on a street with a guy collapsed in a swivel chair before the door of a liquor store. I found myself in front of a shop window with a ring in it costing one cent short of $2000. I found myself surrounded by Hare Krishnas turning circles and playing the world's tiniest cymbals. I found myself in an open space with apartment blocks on all four sides. I found myself staring up at the faces staring down at me. The sun was so hot it had melted into every corner of the square sky. The slightest tear it would all come pouring down and that at last would be that.

Eventually I found myself back at the apartment. The wife beater was there again sitting at the table while Hedda got dinner. You're late she said. Here. Give me a hand.

She had run tonight to a pan – previously uncooked ingredients! – china plates. I trotted where she directed me: yanking open drawers – not that knife the other one … no no the *other* one – boiling kettles draining.

By the time we sat down my head was pounding.

Not even in the last dreadful days before my mother phoned Hedda and begged her to take me off her hands did I eat a quieter meal.

About twenty minutes in your man set his knife and fork down and lit a cigarette. He blew the smoke straight at me then at the last minute reached out a hand and snatched it away – or most of it.

So tell me a bit about yourself.

I stopped chewing – food still in my mouth – trying not to breathe in.

Hedda answered for me. Gem has been a big help since he has been here.

I'll bet he has.

That smirk again.

Hedda slapped the back of his hand: amused you'd have thought rather than offended.

I swallowed at last. Do you know what they used to tell us at primary school? I said.

The boy speaks!

I ignored him. They used to say the worst thing about being a liar wasn't that nobody believed you but that you could never believe anyone else.

God I think they were telling us that when I was there! Hedda touched his hand again – the prelude to a reminiscence. Me and Gem's mummy went to the same school as Gem did she started to say but I cut across her.

Do you think that's why you take me for some sort of scumbag? Because you're such a complete scumbag yourself?

Gem! Hedda's hand shot across from his to mine. I pulled it out of the way.

He finished his draw and blew smoke again into my face. No attempt this time to snatch it back. The smirk twisted into a full-blown sneer.

You told him – right? he said to Hedda. Where the money came from for his ticket here?

To which I wish I had had a better comeback than to topple off my chair.

Vivien was standing a few feet off with her back to me her hands resting palm outwards on her hips which were twitching: to the left to the right to the left to the right. She tossed a glance over her shoulder – winked ... but not at me. Hedda was on my other side: same pose same twitch of the hips same turn of the head and answering wink. My heart was beating in my ears – it was my heart their hips were keeping time with: to the left to the right to the left to the right – wait no – the rhythm I was hearing was coming from behind me rather than within the kick of a drum pedal bolstered by bass guitar. And my own hips were moving too.

Vivien and Hedda turned to face me. There was an electric guitar now too – choppy sounding – and some manner of piano. We clapped our hands stomped our feet taking two steps forward one step back two steps forward one step back until we were within touching distance of one another. We nodded. Now. Another half turn altogether ... Lights came up – bright bright lights. We opened our mouths and oh the joy of joining voices.

Shh–shh–shhh.

Hedda was pressing down on my shoulders easing me back on to the sofa. The light from the lamp on the table next to the arm shone right in my face.

I pushed back against her hands twisting this way and that to get a look at the dining table.

I told him to go on she said.

I lay back again. Sorry I said.

Nothing to be sorry about. I think you must have got a bit too much sun she said. You need to make sure and drink plenty of water. Here.

She lifted a glass from the floor and tilted it to my lips.

I'll be all right now if you want to go on out.

Have you any idea what time it is? You've been gone for the best part of three hours.

I felt like I was stripped down to my underpants beneath the blanket. I turned. My clothes were in a neat pile on the floor.

Was I singing?

Practically non-stop.

Really?

No. Just there now.

Because I dreamed …

What?

I was afraid if I started to speak it it would all fall apart … It doesn't matter.

Do you need me to sit with you a while longer?

I'm OK. Honest.

She reached a hand out up under the lampshade. I meant what I said earlier about you being around you know. It's been good for me.

She turned out the light.

I squeezed my eyes shut trying to summon her voice and Vivien's and mine in harmony but the door was shut on that for the time being. A thin thread of melody that was all I could keep hold of. I hugged it close.

It was morning when I finally woke again. Hedda was standing over me dressed for work. She asked me how I was feeling. I told her: like a different person.

She looked at me doubtfully. Why don't you just stay here today?

I stayed there until I was sure she was down the stairs and out the door then I leapt up.

Really: a different person.

I knew before I saw them that there were boots belonging to me in the very first thrift store I went into that morning. I didn't even have to search too long. They were on a shelf by themselves above a double bay of cowboy boots. Lime green alligator skin (in a universe where alligators were made of plastic). The heels looked like they had come off two different boots. I had to ask the woman at the counter for steps to reach them.

I blew the dust off. Oh that was them all right. I tried the right one on. It went with a bit of forcing.

I think that might actually be a ladies' shoe the woman said.

They're not for me. They're for my sister. We have similarly shaped feet.

Ah.

Twins.

Ah.

She wandered off to serve another customer. I tried on the left one. It didn't remember me half as well as I remembered it.

I took a steak knife from a basket of mismatched cutlery and made a small slit in the seam low down on the heel and tried again and – ha! – on it went. As easy as that.

Who even looked down there anyway?

All the same I made a slit in the right one too just to even it up.

I gave the woman her dollar fifty.

I hope your sister likes the boots she said.

Oh she's going to love them.

The trousers I had left in the bargain bin inside the door of another place just off 96th Street: 75c it cost me to get them back. A bit more of a flare than I remembered but that could be easily fixed too and they were definitely the right shade of pink. (Hedda had of course been wrong about the colour combinations being exhausted.) All the labels had been taken off so there was no way of knowing what exactly they were made of although I thought it would probably be wise to avoid naked flames high wattage bulbs – even direct sunlight.

I had one white T-shirt to my name. Whitish. It looked better if you turned it inside out. Itched less too without the stitching against my armpits. I'm not selling this get-up very well but take my word for it: it was pretty fucking deadly. I nearly gave myself the horn.

Even with the slits the boots weren't the easiest to walk in. Actually they were murder. For some reason long strides hurt less but still after every couple of dozen I would have to take a breather. During one of these – I hadn't gone more than five hundred yards from the apartment – a car slowed. It was about four of my giant strides long. I know because as soon as it stopped I starting walking again. A barrage of noise came from the inside. The driver leaned a bare arm in the frame of the open window. Shit little brother you're in a pretty bad way there.

I'm fine. Thanks.

How far you going?

Not far.

He kept pace with me for half a block. I took another pause. So did he.

Why don't you get in?

Seriously I'm fine.

The front seat passenger leaned across him. He had a match in his mouth that he moved from one side to the other before he spoke. The man is offering you a ride here. Get in the car.

The driver himself reached behind him and opened the door. There was another guy already in the back not much bigger than me but with a heavy moustache. He wore orange-tinted sunglasses and a sleeveless denim jacket with nothing on underneath. A patch in the shape of a light bulb on the left breast pocket said *I'm A Fucking Genius*. He had a large portable cassette player on his lap. I had no words at all for the music coming out of it: the speed of the guitars the percussion ... He turned it up the moment we started to drive again. I thought I might have a heart attack.

No need to look so scared the guy in the passenger seat said.

I'm not.

Could have fooled me. This is our good deed for the day he said then laughed slapping the outside of the car.

The driver angled the mirror so he could see me. He narrowed his eyes.

I'm trying to work it out whereabouts you're from.

Ireland I said. I had given up on the Northern.

He turned in his seat. The car veered towards the kerb until his passenger – co-pilot make that – reached out a hand and steadied the wheel.

You mean like *Belfast*?

What do you know? Yeah I said. I mean exactly Belfast.

The driver cuffed the co-pilot with the back of his hand. Hear that? Belfast! To me again: That's some tough city.

It sounded as though he was congratulating me.

I suppose it can be. (What else was I going to say?)

The guy beside me pushed his glasses up one-fingered to look at me again in the light of this new information. He laid his upturned palm out on the seat between us. I looked at it a moment uncertain then laid my own on top of it. He crooked his fingers gripping mine. Respect.

So where can we take you? the driver said.

I told him West 74th Street. If you're sure it's no trouble.

No trouble at all! You're our guest.

We stopped along the way to pick up some liquor – five-glass bottles I would have called them – curved to fit against ribs – stopped again while the guy beside me got out and ran into an apartment house – that's his nanna's the driver said obviously not caring that it sounded like a lie – and came out again a couple of minutes later wearing a different pair of sunglasses and stuffing something into the pocket with the light bulb on it.

How is your nanna? the driver asked.

She's doing good the guy said without missing a beat. So who knows?

In between times all they wanted to talk about was the war back home. Man how they would love to come over and help us take on those Brits: were they using gunships and shit against us?

There were helicopters yes I said.

Right right that's what they meant.

It was hard sometimes to get to sleep.

There was a pause. Then right right they said again.

What I wanted to say to them was that my mother and I had already had to leave one house because of the church we didn't even go to – that I had stopped wearing clothes so I couldn't be made to go out – that every single thing had started to frighten me because every single random crash or bang sounded like the prelude to a bomb or gun attack and every single place looked like a news report waiting to happen – that *weird* seemed to me a better word to have hurled at you than *dead*.

I'm OK just here I said when we were coming up on 74th.

You sure? the driver said. We can leave you to your door.

You would have to turn left.

Left is no trouble. He demonstrated. The driver behind sounded his horn then as the guy beside me leaned half his body out to yell a Go fuck yourself man seemed instantly to want to take it back: you could nearly hear the suck of it.

Honestly here is fine.

So there was where we stopped at a forty-five-degree angle to the junction.

We did a round of the hand-clasping thing back seat and front.

You take good care of yourself now the driver said. Hear?

I heard all right. He reached behind again and opened the door. His car his decision when you went and when you stayed.

The car started to pull away. Then stopped again at forty-five degrees in the other direction. (Not a peep or a beep from the car behind.) The driver beckoned me. I leaned in again. Everyone over there dress like that? he asked.

I'd say it's kind of fifty–fifty.

He nodded. All three raised their fists out their windows as they drove off. I raised mine in return.

The photographs you never get.

However it had happened the boots had become more bearable while I was sitting in the car. Stepping out on to the road I could take short steps or long no bother. If I could have done the splits I could have done the splits.

You know what you can do though I said to myself out of absolutely nowhere: you can go out to Queens – to Cambria Heights.

So that was what I did.

On the subway.

With all the other normal New York people who it turned out were too busy reading their books and their newspapers or leaning their heads on their lovers' shoulders or staring into space to want to rob or kill me.

The carriage was a dump but at least it didn't smell of piss like some of the buses at home.

I had to get off at 42nd Street and look around in the underground passages for one that led me to the E train. I realised I was lost when I passed a guy for the second time in one of the landings sitting on a blanket selling what looked like the contents of somebody's bin. I doubled back. In among the debris and the sign saying *Trying To Get Home* was a pocket instamatic camera.

Does the camera work?

(I was still thinking of photos never got.)

What do you think I am? Of course it works.

How much?

Five dollars.

It's too much.

It has a flashcube already on it.

They're all used.

OK four.

Sorry. Not interested.

You can take the cube off.

I tried. I couldn't: It's stuck.

Three fifty then.

I gave him two plus some change and asked him to point me to the E train.

I was down on the platform before I noticed that the camera was already loaded. Three shots taken. I told myself when it was developed I would go back and give the guy his pictures. And maybe something extra for the film.

An hour and more I was on the train to where it ended in a place called Jamaica. Already the city and its skyscrapers looked as distant as Oz. Looked more like a week than an hour away. And I still had further to go – by bus now: a grimmer proposition as it turned out than the subway. Another half an hour. All the way (I asked the driver for the stop closest to Andrew Jackson High School) to Francis Lewis Boulevard.

You know that school's out don't you? the guy in the seat behind the driver's said and laughed turning his head inviting the other passengers to join in.

He hadn't a single tooth in his head.

He shouted it again as I was getting off. You're a couple a weeks too early! Or a couple a months too late. I heard him through the slowly closing doors call down the bus. I'm telling him he's a couple a weeks too early!

The school was vast. White stone front and leaded windows and grand gateposts with lanterns on top.

I asked a large woman out walking a small dog to take a photograph of me in front of the gate.

We went through the where-I-was-from chat.

You came all this way to visit? Who knew we were so famous? Tell me what I'm supposed to press here. The Shangri-Las? (I managed to get it out.) Oh I haven't heard that name in years! Are you sure they went to Andrew Jackson? I went here myself: Class of '43. Happy days. Oh sure there was the *War* but when you're that age all that seems so far away. (I wondered had she been walking up and down all day waiting for someone to talk to.) Turn your head a little to the right ... back towards me a touch ... that's better.

Her dog had walked to the end of its lead and sat down to have a pee. Pure Gatorade.

She gave me the camera back. Smile-sighed. Happy happy days.

I wandered around the grounds a bit trying to imagine the sisters with their books clutched tight to their chests: oh hi Margie – hi Mary Ann – hi you – hi you – how was the ... ah ... the ... ah ... ah ... you know ...

Only I didn't know – couldn't begin to imagine at all. What did they talk about?

I turned a corner.

Boys.

Playing basketball on an outdoor court maybe fifty yards away. It was hard to tell how many exactly. They were moving fast weaving in and out. The tallest of them plucked the looping ball out of the sky just short of the painted line and jumped with it towards the hoop then seemed to change his mind in mid-air. He landed ball balanced against his hip looking at me. *The fuck is he staring*

at? The others who had been defending the hoop stopped
too and turned in my direction. They looked at the tall
one again as if for instruction. Then – I realised they were
going to a split second before they did – they all started to
run. I beat it back round the corner where there was a door.
I don't know why I thought it would open but I pushed it
anyway and – wonder of wonders – it did. I ran on past. I
was round the next corner before the boys arrived. One of
them shouted: *He must have gone in here – I heard a door.*
I heard it again as they opened it. I heard their sneakers
slapping and squeaking on tiled stairs. I found my way out
the front again. A woman called to me: Irish boy! It was
the woman who had taken the photograph. I ran to her.
Her dog was rearing up on its twiggy legs lead straining
front paws paddling the air in front of my thigh. So after I
talked to you I went straight to the call box over there and
called my cousin Sarah the woman said. Sarah's daughter
Angela was a freshman in 1962: she knew those girls. She
thinks they lived about 220th Street. I could walk you.
It's just across the Boulevard here. She pointed in the
direction the heaviest traffic sound was coming from.

You know what that's really kind of you I said – I
could see behind her the boys emerging from up the side
of the main building. I kept her between them and me as
we talked – but maybe it's best to leave a bit of mystery
not spoil all the magic.

The woman shook her head slowly: respect for my
maturity – sorrow that it was shared by so few of my age
or maybe sex. You are so right she said. You are so so so

right. The dog swivelled on its lead and started barking. The woman turned. Are those your friends? she asked. The basketball boys had me in their sights again. How anyone could have taken their looks for friendly was beyond me. I think they think I'm someone else I said and before the woman could turn again I took advantage of a last-gasp *WALK* sign to skip across the street. Cars poured into the road behind me. In the movie there would have been a Jamaica bus arriving. I would have sat at the back throwing V-signs as the boys fell further and further behind. It being life I had to make do with bolting into a diner next to the first bus stop I came to half a block away where I sat down at a table beside a couple still young enough to be my parents and asked them for their menu then asked them to point out stuff they'd recommend then spent money I hadn't wanted to on a piece of pie the size of my head topped off with a pompadour of canned whipped cream.

Which had just been set in front of me when the boys from the school arrived outside looking angrier than ever.

The Lord only knows what I had done to upset them so much. Except maybe look good. I told the couple how nice the pie was and told them again every time they looked away from me and tried to restart their conversation. (From what I could gather it related to her work: she really thought they were taking her for granted you know?) The boys hung around a while longer weighing it up – weighing the couple and me up. Maybe they really were my parents. Maybe they had been sitting here all this time waiting for me to finish wandering around Andrew Jackson High. Eventually the boys got bored and drifted off.

A minute or two later the couple at the table with me got up and left. (I wanted to tell her I appreciated her even if nobody else did. You know?) I pushed my plate away. I felt as though I had eaten a brick. I'd missed at least three buses too. By the time I got back to Jamaica switched from bus to train and made it into 42nd Street and from 42nd to 110th by way of another train that didn't seem in too much of a hurry to get anywhere any time soon it was already as close to dark as it ever got. Dark and humid. I closed my eyes as I stepped out of the station feeling the thickness clogging my mouth and nose. The thought flashed through my mind: this is what the grave would feel like.

Hedda threatened for the first time in a long time that night to send me back home to mine.

She turned towards the door as I walked in through it. She looked as though she had been pacing. She looked like my mother.

Where the hell have you been?

You're not going to believe this I said and told her the whole story – or the whole of it from I got out of the car at 74th Street and playing down the boys who followed me to the diner: the woman with the dog – Sarah her cousin – Angela Sarah's daughter – the Andrew Jackson High School.

She shook her head. The seam of my right boot had gone completely. My heel was sticking out: filthy. (Well there was no way I could have fitted a sock between it and the boot.) I don't know what had happened to the trousers. They were cracked – corrugated. Apparently even body heat was more than they could cope with.

I think you are maybe taking this a bit far.

I laughed short and sharp. Of course I am. I thought that was the whole point. Everybody's taking everything too far. At least I'm taking something beautiful. What the fuck are you doing?

Don't you ever – she said starting slowly gathering force – raise your voice to me in *my* house.

It's not your house: it's his!

Something flew through the air – I saw it just in time to jerk my head to one side – and struck the wall behind me.

An ashtray.

She actually threw an ashtray at me. Tin. Not that she checked first. The closest thing to her right hand was all. If she had led with her left – where the glass ashtray sat – they could have been burying me right there in Manhattan.

A silence opened up in the aftermath swallowing us both.

Hedda broke it slamming the bedroom door.

Fuck her.

I struggled out of my boots – the left one ripped the whole way up to the top seam – and lay down on the sofa. Arms folded knees pulled up face to the back cushion.

And that was how I woke eight hours later thinking *Shit what did I say?*

There was a black smudge on the wall where the ashtray had hit. Butts were scattered still across the lino a swathe cut through them where Hedda had yanked the door open on her way out of the apartment. I picked each butt up by hand. I would have picked them up lit and held them in my fist to prove how sorry I was. Look. *Look.*

When I had finished there I went into the bathroom and started to put everything back together: rewinding the clock to the moment before she came in here this morning – still raging with me most likely – and blew the place apart. I binned the debris shone up the chrome taps and wiped down the tiles.

I went out to buy flowers.

As I was going down the stairs Mrs Mogilevich was coming up them. Slowly. And with shopping. Here I said and took the bag from her. Let me give you a hand. She tried to give me a dollar for my trouble. It's all right I said.

I know she said but take it. Maybe you could come down some other day and help me with some stuff.

The dollar passed back and forth a couple of times more before I gave in and added it to the two I already had in my pocket and bought half as many flowers again as I thought I could afford: purple whirligigs and chrysanthemums and some make of rose. I arranged them in a vase on the table and prepared an apology in my head for when Hedda came home.

But Hedda didn't come home. I sat and waited until after midnight then swung my legs up on to the sofa and went to sleep again.

I woke to find her staring down at me. There was light coming in at the window behind which only made her expression darker. I shrank back into my pillow. I thought she might have the other ashtray in her hand.

It's all over she said. Are you happy now? I need you to know though – that scar of mine? – I fell. I was taking pills then. Never ever ever take pills. Hear? I was right out of it. He came in and found me. I'd been lying with my back against a pipe. Couple of hours they reckon. He got me to the hospital. And that was him gone.

She went into the bathroom and came out again twenty minutes later dressed for work. Don't touch a thing in there she said before she left.

The next few days were awful. We managed to be civil when we couldn't avoid meeting but avoidance seemed far and away the best policy. I spent more time down in Mrs Mogilevich's apartment giving her a hand clearing out her ex-husband's belongings. His clothes consisted of identical suits in three colours – grey blue and brown: worsted for winter cotton for summer. It was hard to imagine the man I had known ever filling them.

She showed me a photograph. Mr Mogilevich – the eyes were about all I recognised – linking arms with another young man squinting out from a long-ago Russian summer's day.

His mother sent him for English lessons in secret Mrs M said. The village where he lived the council – soviet: that was all that word meant – were denouncing people left right and centre. Well right and centre anyway. The other young man in that photograph? Mr M's friend since before they both could walk. The secret police came to his door one night and took him away.

Next morning Mr M started walking.

He arrived in New York four months later speaking the language better than the men who were waiting to greet him. They could hardly believe the story he told them – what he had to go through to reach there. He never talked about it again to anyone but her after that day.

Nineteen-twenty-four. Another year he might not have got out at all. And then where would Mrs M have been? Who would Mrs M have been?

I always told him he was lucky to get me she said but the luck was all mine.

I thought of the old man shuffling to the apartment door every time he heard a foot on the stairs. I had one of those flashes such as you only get (or such as at least as I have only had) a handful of times in the course of your life the absolute inescapable fact that death is not a recessive gene skipping a generation: *your* generation and you as the ultimate expression of your generation.

As you are he once was. As he is you will be.

His smile! Mrs M said. I had been married to him a year before I found out his teeth were made entirely of wood. Of wood? I said thinking I had maybe misheard – or she had. But she was insistent. He had done them himself – the springs and all. He had new teeth made eventually here in New York – the finest porcelain – but they were never as good as the wooden ones … you never saw a smile to match it. Russian birch.

One afternoon she gave me a bag with twenty-three of his ties in it. Maybe they are not so fashionable now she said. She pulled one out. Alternating wine and silver chevrons with what looked like three headless jumbo shrimp battling blindly to the top. I put it on to please her. It smelled (don't ask me to explain) of disappointment.

You can give them all away if you want.

I brought them back up to Hedda's and laid them out on the floor trying to work out a chronology – where did the knitted one fit? And this one with the ducks?

A life in neckties. A few were the worse for wear others barely worn at all. One was still in its protective polythene sheath. The design was a woman in her underwear hands clasped behind her head: *$2.50* the tag on the back said.

I sat back on the sofa to survey my handiwork. Pulled my feet up and turned so that I could stretch out.

The television was all *Voyager II* which had been launched the day before on its way to Jupiter and Saturn and eventually in 2017 out of the solar system altogether. I felt for a moment – between the ties and the television commentary – precisely poised.

A key turned in the lock and the door slammed open. Hedda home already. Early-summer Hedda: barely holding her excitement in.

They're playing at CBGB.

I hauled myself upright. Something ran under the icebox in the kitchen. It barely fizzed on me.

Playing as in performing? (I didn't need to ask who *They* were.) Like standing up and singing?

Tonight. Margie told me herself.

All that time I'd hung around there on the footpath when I would have been better off standing behind the counter of the deli.

She nearly spilled her change she was bouncing that much Hedda said. They just decided. They were all running off to ring their friends.

I stood up from the sofa. Hedda was looking at the ties.

What's CBGB?

No idea.

She heaved out the phone directory. Flop – open … wrong place. Flop flop flop again. Flick flick flick flick … flick back …

Oh crap.

What?

Nothing. She shut the directory and shoved it back on the shelf. Go get on you.

There was nowhere for me to go but I got on me all right the moment she closed her bedroom door. You bet I did.

The boots were fucked but the trousers would go another turn. The T-shirt too. I kept on the tie with the jumbo shrimp on it.

Hedda came out in a pair of denim shorts and a satin college jacket. I hadn't seen either of them before.

Lose the tie she said. Or better yet …

She loosened the knot enough to slip it over my head and down on to her own where she tugged it tight again. There.

We rode downtown – Hedda taking the subway! – down down – changed at Columbus Circle – *down*town. The carriage emptied and re-filled three times over: 42nd – 34th – 14th – 34th – 14th. There was another more or less total evacuation at West 4th Street. Only one person got on. He looked as though he had been pulled out from the rubble of a collapsed building. A wildness in his eyes after so long staring into the void. A bottle in a brown paper bag that he drank from as soon as he sat down making up for lost time then passed out limbs sprawled.

Hedda nudged me. Our stop.

We had to clamber over the man's legs. I stepped on to the platform. Looked back. Hedda had her hand on his shoulder. The eyes – reopened – were wilder even than before. They saw the five-dollar bill in Hedda's other hand the same moment I did the moment before the doors started to shut and she hopped minus five dollars out of the carriage.

Maybe that was the real reason she never came down here. She would have emptied her purse every journey she took.

We walked the short distance from the station to the Bowery: as far removed then from the origins of its name as any place on the disfigured face of this planet.

The guy who passed out in our carriage had only been a harbinger. Here was the epicentre of whatever disaster had struck although up here it had more the character of war. Casualties lay strewn across the footpath half in half out of doorways pools around this one or that of their – or their bottles' – making. There was a smell in the air of burning: several generations of it.

Hand on heart? No matter what the attraction at the end of it if Hedda hadn't been with me I'd probably have skittered back the way I came.

Hedda must have sensed my hesitation. We're not turning round now she said.

We would have found the club even without the awning out front. It was just about the only place on the entire block at that time of the night that wasn't chained shut or boarded up. A handful of guys in drainpipes and beat-up tennis shoes stood smoking at the door. A dog – hound – shaggy of coat pointed of muzzle wriggled out nearly taking the legs from under one of them. It had a look up and down the street lifted its own leg a couple of times without issue and ran back towards the guys who had the sense this time to part. Hedda and I followed through the dog-cleared channel – me the whole time waiting for a hand on the shoulder that didn't come. Hedda did all the talking to the young woman in the biker jacket on the other side of the door. I was from Ireland nobody carried ID there: the wrong people found out who you were – what you were – you could wind up lying in a ditch with a bullet in the back of your head … so you know if the woman wanted to punish me for not getting myself *killed* … Besides she was my big sister (that made me smile): she could vouch for me.

The word had gone out late. It was a Sunday night the fag end of summer. I doubt there were more than a hundred people in there besides Hedda and me. In the years since I have read the names of some people who said they were. I wouldn't have known then who I was looking at nor could I now conjure a likeness with who they turned out to be but I will take their word for it. Just as they will have to take mine. They might remember Hedda. That old Russian man's headless shrimp tie round her nut like what else would a person have there?

We moved through them to what looked like a clear space but turned out to be a table – there didn't seem to be any chairs went with it – that was more a staging post where people set their drinks or occasionally rested their cigarettes (one – left and forgotten – had turned to a cylinder of ash) before pushing forward to see what was happening at the front which at that moment was not a lot.

The stage if you could call it that was low and in a kind of recess: a couple of fluorescent tubes – like the one in the kitchen at home in Belfast – with a handful of spotlights thrown in at random. One complete side of it was floor-to-ceiling posters. A moustachioed man in a straw boater – hands jammed in his trouser pockets – looking out at me across an unfathomable century (where would you even begin?) a woman next to him in a world and a poster of her own dancing with her arms laced above her head. Another woman beside her with flowers in the bodice of her dress.

The instruments looked like they had been left there for whoever felt like it to pick up and use – guitar drums a funny little bass that might have been bumping from place to place since the Beatles first passed through town.

The only music was coming from a jukebox which when we entered was playing something I couldn't catch enough of to put a name to but have since convinced myself was the Everly Brothers. Love Hurts sounds about right.

Hedda bought us both a beer. The whole summer I was there that was the only alcohol to pass my lips. It tasted of something by which I don't mean a thing whose precise name eluded me I mean it actually had a taste – a not unpleasant one either – which was not an accusation you could have levelled at the beers I had previously forced down my neck. It was cold too; straight out of the fridge. You could nearly understand it as a drink connected to thirst and not just picking fights.

I tipped the bottle up this one moment tilting my head and the jukebox cut out – cheers rose all around me – and when I lowered the bottle they were there on the stage in the same outfits pretty much that I had seen them in coming and going from the studio all these weeks: jeans and shirts for the sisters a halterneck for Margie each walking to her mic as though they had been doing it without interruption since they walked for the last time out the gates of Andrew Jackson High.

Thank you all so much for coming Mary said.

It was a voice I could have heard in any street or shop in the city. You have a nice day. That'll be four dollars fifty. Sir you can't go in there.

She had her glasses on and then – I must have been looking straight at her and still missed it – she didn't and Liz did.

This was kind of a last-minute arrangement she said. She stepped away from the microphone and instantly stepped back: Well if you call from 1967 last minute. And then the band – the band? it was Andy and some friends who had wandered on behind the girls – the band kicked in and Mary Weiss with just the slightest scrunch of her face was singing: I got a guy name of Bony Maronie ... he's as skinny as a stick of macaroni ... I wanted everything to go slower let me take every note every syllable of it in and I didn't want it to let up for a second. Some guy – Bony's build but maybe longer – had started jumping up and down in front of the stage to something in the music no one else could hear. The Shangri-Las clustered around a single microphone then in the next instant moved apart Margie to the left Liz to the right as nonchalantly as choosing a car door. Already I was imagining myself telling this back to someone – don't ask me who – Vivien maybe wherever she was: *And Andy was in that leather jacket of his and the guy playing the Beatley bass had long hair – I mean like hippy long – the drummer too – and the Shangri-Las – I swear to God – the Shangri-Las were ten feet from where I was standing and their voices were like the three parts of the one immense thing ...*

Hedda put her arm round my shoulder. It's all right she said which was the first I knew that I was crying. I'm not upset I said. I'm I'm … I didn't know what the word even was. I don't know if I know it yet. Hedda told me she knew without me having to say it anyway. Really she said amid the whistling and cheering and stomping that greeted the end of the song – it's all right.

Mary had started telling a story about being on the road in Georgia way back when: some guys trying to break down the door of her hotel room in the middle of the night. Margie and Liz sitting on the speakers wagged their heads at one another smiling wryly: *remember that night?* Mary in her story was off out first thing next morning to buy herself a gun.

We were teenagers she said. Out there on our own. I mean it shouldn't have been allowed. She looked over her shoulder: left then right then to some third place where I could have imagined Mary Ann once stood. Margie and Liz caught the drift of her eyes. Nodded. Wryless.

Our *bodyguard* was a teenager Mary said turning again – pulling herself and the other girls back from the contemplation of that absence. Poor guy had barely been out of New York before. Barely even been out of Queens.

A young woman in a biker jacket – camera in her hand – went into a crouch beside me. I thought she might have been the same woman that was taking money at the door earlier. It was difficult to tell with the camera in front of her face.

I looked behind me. No Hedda: this way that way. Then I saw her – back up at the bar leaning so far forward

her feet must have been right off the ground talking to
an older woman standing next to a big guy with a beard
who was holding on to the two beers he had been going
to hand to Hedda and who I realised then was also – in
between listening to her – looking over at me and shaking
his head.

I faced forward again – gave myself over entirely
to Mary.

She and the rest of the band and the bodyguard who
would have needed a bodyguard of his own had travelled
by bus from Georgia down to Florida where Mary
hopped off at the first station house they came to and
handed her gun in to the cops. Which might she said have
been the only time in the history of the Twenty-seventh
State that anyone had voluntarily surrendered a firearm.
The drummer ba-domed his bass drum and crashed the
cymbals. The audience whistled and cheered some more.
Margie and Liz were on their feet again running their
hands down their legs as they took up their positions.

Hedda came back without the beers. I could read her
face every last mole and eyelash. I didn't want her to have
to be the one to say it so I said it for her. I think maybe
this would be a good time to leave.

Andy and the longhaired bass player started it

Oo-oo-oo-oo-oo a passable falsetto that Margie and
Liz reinforced – *ooo* – before the drummer applied his
foot to the pedal pedal to the drum. Hedda and I pushed
back through the audience – Watch! – stepped over the
dog stretched out with its head on its paws and reached

the doors. Only then did I look back. A blue gauze curtain had fallen between the Shangri-Las and me: a trick of smoke and lights and the moisture in the air. Their faces – the musicians' faces – had lost all definition. I heard the voices though clear as a pristine record above the bass above the guitar and the drums and the noise that even a hundred people hanging on every word can't help but make.

He don't hang around with the gang no more

And he don't do the wild things that he did before.

We were carried Hedda and I by the rising *oos* – Margie's and Liz's (Andy and the bass player knew better than to even try to keep up) until –

He used to act bad he used to but he quit it – we arrived – It makes me so sad – where the lyric had been leading us where Mary's boy's heart was –

out in the streets

New York city night

August 1977

Elvis dead and gone to his rest in a cavalcade of white limousines.

And I knew that they did it for me.

Let's walk I said.

I was down on West 74th Street as usual the next day. I strolled up and down until past noon. Not a sinner – or at least not a Shangri-La – turned up at Number 165 which on the morning after the night before was only to be expected. Not a one turned up the next day either or the day after that. The guy with the granny specs went in late in the afternoon and a matter of minutes later came out again.

He stood on the steps looking up and down the street like where to now?

I thought this is my last chance. I crossed over.

Kid he said.

And I said I do have a song.

He came down to my level fixing his glasses on the bridge of his nose. You have?

It's called Keep the Faith.

Sounds like a psalm … That's not a bad thing. I mean if the rest of the song is in the same vein – organs maybe.

He stood in front of me head to one side. And stood.

What?

Well let me hear it.

You mean sing it? Right here?

A song's natural element the open air. Gershwin said that.

I had hoped I would at least make it in the door before I had to open my mouth but there was nothing else for it now. I closed my eyes and tried to block out everything but the memory of the call-it-dream call-it-vision I'd had the night I fell from the chair – my voice joined with Vivien's and Hedda's: that one note we had hit. Start there. Let all you have listened to and lived these weeks in this city be your guide. I couldn't quite believe how easily it came together verse into verse into chorus. When I opened my eyes again he was looking at me jaw hanging. I thought this could go either way.

Oh kid.

It went that way.

He covered his eyes with his hands pushing the specs up on to his forehead dragged his fingers down his cheeks again.

I really thought for a minute that was going to be good he said. Which is a shame because you have something. Not looks – good grief no – but a thing going on – that's for sure. People have made it with a lot less.

He shrugged. And sometimes he said – I thought maybe he was no longer addressing just me – it doesn't matter what you have it's just not your moment.

He held out his fist. I pressed mine to it. And off he walked.

A week later I was back in Belfast and sitting at a desk with *Stranglers* gouged into the wood beneath the inkwell taking down my sixth-year timetable from the blackboard.

My mother had rung the evening of my impromptu audition. Right she said it's time to come home.

I asked Hedda: Did you put her up to this?

She's your mother. She doesn't need me to put her up to anything.

Which I took to mean yes she probably did.

I went downstairs to Mrs Mogilevich. You're doing the right thing she said. Go to school. You can never have too much learning.

I sat out next morning on the island in the middle of Broadway watching the taxis rush towards me on my left and away from me on my right. Either it was getting cooler finally or I was getting used to the heat. I stuck it longer than I had managed all the time I had been there.

Hedda had asked me if I wanted anything special from the deli for dinner my last night in New York. I didn't even have to think.

We sat down facing one another across a carton of noodles and another of eggplant with its black bean spawn.

She raised her balloon glass to me. You can come back any time. I raised my Coke. You never know I might just.

At the airport I kept trying to tell her I'm all right here I'm all right here – I couldn't be sure I wasn't going to cry again – but she came with me in the end almost as far as the gate. At the last minute she reached into the shoulder bag she was carrying and pulled out a brown-paper-wrapped package a foot and a bit squared an eighth of an inch thick.

Gee I said like I had been saying it all my life. I wonder what that could be.

There's cardboard around it to protect it she said.

You mean in case the plane comes down?

That's not even funny.

She hugged me. As tight as tight. Go.

All that autumn I listened to the radio obsessively searching out those slivers of bandwidth where I thought the Shangri-Las might first appear: those same slivers where to begin with I found the Ramones – Richard Hell – Patti Smith – the Dead Boys – Bowery breakouts all.

My mother said she was sorry she had ever complained about Radio 3. Please – any time you like – switch back. She stopped just short of telling me I could take all my clothes off again. I read the music papers too – *NME Melody Maker & Sounds* – the snippets as well as the two-page spreads but with every week that passed I listened and read with less and less expectation.

Then early the following year a few photographs from the night at CBGB turned up with as little fanfare as the night itself in one of the papers I forget which – poor reproductions shrunken indistinct – with nothing to indicate that the gig they showed was already more than five months old. (I remembered the young woman in the biker jacket dropping into a crouch in front of the stage.) I knew then for sure that what took place that night – in the weeks leading up to it – was in the eyes of all but a very few without any kind of consequence.

A while later the Paley Brothers LP came out. Andy and Jonathan on the cover: white shirts blue jeans against a red-brick wall. Blond and blonder handsome and handsomer – him and him-er.

I bought it of course. I don't know how many other people did. Not enough for a second record anyway.

I still listen to it now and again – Baby baby you're the best: better better than all the rest (did you hear that Vivien?) – like I listen to Walk Away Renée: with something close to awe. Now and again too I take out the *Golden Hits of The Shangri-Las*. Not the one that Vivien brought with her to the apartment the morning we lied ourselves calm enough to fuck though that's here too. The other one with the pops and skips and glides and with – I discovered when I unpicked the Sellotape from the brown paper as my plane lifted off from New York four decades ago – an inner sleeve purloined from another record entirely (*Atlantic Stereo 8000 series*) a note on it in Hedda's hand. *To Gem. Keep this ... and keep the Youknowwhat.*

And well there's been some shit – there is shit even as I am writing this – and Times Square now is worse than Times Square then and I still haven't worked out whether I am travelling towards my moment or hurtling away from it but you know what? I have tried Hedda. I have tried.

Not one of the photographs I took the day I caught the train and the bus to Queens came out in the end. All I got back from the developers in fact were the three shots the guy who sold me the camera had already taken. The first is of a light fitting the second of a back yard – snow on the ground: a child's bicycle lying on its side the rubber grip missing from the left handle.

The third photo is of the man himself lying on a sofa shirt off arms folded across his chest: asleep. No idea perhaps that it was even being taken or what was coming down the line for him.

I am sorry to this day I didn't give him the four dollars he asked for.

I hope he found his way back.